Punishing for Pleasure

Masters of the Prairie Winds Club
Book Five

by Avery Gale

Dedication

To my readers...I'm sharing with you the note I attached to the hand-embroidered handkerchief I gave my youngest son on his wedding day...

Prologue

Four Weeks Earlier…

ASH LOOKED AT the gorgeous submissive secured in the rope swing and marveled at her flexibility. *Yes indeed, there is a lot to be said for yoga.* Mary Dillon's pussy was engorged with blood from her arousal and glistened brightly as her cream coated the sensitive tissues in preparation for them. He and Dex had blindfolded her during the time they'd stripped her naked and secured her open for all to see in the rope swing. More than one submissive had assured him the apparatus was actually extremely comfortable despite the fact it looked like some sort of Middle Ages torture device.

One of Mary's hot points was her intimidation about public play and nudity. Neither he nor Dex had been able to figure out exactly what was at the root of her discomfort, but since it didn't seem to be out-right fear, they were determined to help her move past it. They'd kept her eyes covered during the first part of her flogging, but had removed the black silk mask when her soft moans had indicated she was well beyond caring. Since tonight was the first time they were going to fuck her together, it was important they be able to monitor her reactions closely. And as the ancients often quoted, "The eyes are the windows to the soul".

Sliding the silk fabric from her unfocused eyes, Ash smiled into her dazed expression, "Pet, you are doing so well, I'm very proud of you." Her lips curved up into a sensuous smile that told him on some level she'd processed his words of praise. *God she is fucking gorgeous and submissive to the core.* He loved the way she responded equally to both he and Dex. So often the women they'd shared had seemed to connect with one of them more than the other, and they'd always known that would never work for them long-term so they'd kept looking. Finding Mary had been by pure blessed coincidence.

Bringing his focus back to the lush woman in front of him, Ash saw Dex step up to the control panel mounted on the wall. Ash cupped her chin to center her focus on him as he spoke, "Mary, Master Dex is going to move you into position now." The controls were so finely tuned the movement was gentle and smooth, but he knew it was still disorienting for her when he heard her small gasp. They didn't want to pull her back too much, so he leaned forward and covered her lips with his own. He'd taken advantage of that sweet gasp and slid his tongue deep without any resistance at all. Ash let the fingers of one hand slide slowly down her neck and over her shoulder. The intensity of the kiss seemed to morph from a casual attempt to distract her to full-on possession in the time it took his heart to beat. He could smell her arousal and moved his hand in a slow slide down her torso until his fingers were sliding between the slick folds of her pussy.

"Oh, my pretty pet, you are so wet and I can't tell you how much that pleases us." Sliding his fingers through the slick folds of her sex, listening to the wet sounds, and seeing her bright green eyes dilate so fully that there was little more than a tiny ring of color left showing, it was straight out of his hottest fantasies. *Fuck me, she is gorgeous.* "Are you ready, pet? Master Dex is going to start working the lube into your tight little asshole. You've done so well with the plugs, and now we're going to show you all the delicious pleasures of a true ménage." Ash paused for several seconds to let his words settle in.

He knew the minute Dex's well-lubed fingers began rimming her tender tissues. Her eyes widened just before her eyelids slid down, as if they were chasing her soft moan. Her head rolled back, too heavy for her to hold up any longer. "Mary, look at me." She struggled to bring her head back up but didn't appear to have enough focus to make her muscles cooperate. "Now, pet, or we'll stop right here. We'll simply take you down and you'll miss all the pleasure we have planned for you."

Dex looked over her delicate shoulder and grinned. "Sweetness, you best follow those instructions because I'm going to be mighty unhappy if I don't get to slide into this tight little ass. Feeling your body gripping my cock with the rippling strength you're using on my fingertips is going to blow my mind." Dex leaned forward and opened his mouth over the sweet spot where her shoulders and neck met, closing just enough to know his teeth would mark her tawny skin. They'd learned that spot and just above the dimples of her ass were particularly sensitive for their sweet subbie. Ash watched as Dex bit down and then laved the mark he'd left with his tongue. "Open those gorgeous green eyes, baby, because I'm not sure I could stop now if I wanted to. My cock is about to burst for wanting to sink into you."

Ash watched as her eyes slowly opened. *So fucking perfect.* She was willing to put forth the effort for her Master when she hadn't been able to step back from the edge for her own pleasure. "Pet, we are going to send you so high you are going to swear you heard the angels sing." He'd opened his leathers and rolled on a condom while Dex had been playing with her and now Ash heard the distinctive crinkle of a condom wrapper, watching Dex for his quick nod. When it came, Ash wrapped his arms around Mary, picking her up just a bit. Feeling the shudders rippling through her was just about the sexiest thing he'd ever felt. "Tell me." When Mary's eyes started to roll back, Ash gave her a quick squeeze and repeated the words, this time putting more command behind them. It fascinated him how she responded to soft and gentle outside of BDSM play, but during scenes, her submission was directly proportional to the Master's ability to command.

"It's so hot. I mean, it burns when he stretches it, but it's more than that too. It's naughty, but in such a delicious way." Ash saw Dex set the lube aside and knew she was ready to take them both even if she wasn't going to think so for a few minutes.

DEX PULLED HER lush ass cheeks apart so he could watch as the tip of his cock pushed against her puckered hole. Seeing a part of himself entering her most intimate place did something to his heart that he couldn't even begin to understand. He felt her tighten against him and knew the reaction had been pure reflex, but he gave her ass a sharp slap anyway. "Don't you dare try to keep me out, sweetness, it won't work, and it will just rob you of the pleasure." He didn't mention it would just make his pleasure more intense, and when she relaxed, he softened his tone, "There's a good girl, take a deep breath and push back just a bit." Dex saw her back bow in a graceful arch as she pushed back against him, or at least as much as Ash's hold would allow. He began working his way inside her ass with barely leashed control. The heat of her body quickly surrounded the tip and, for a heartbeat or two, Dex wondered if he was going to survive the next half hour. By the time he'd worked all the way in, she was squeezing him hard enough that he worried he might not be able to hold back his own release.

"Oh my God and Sister Gertrude. I have to come, please let me come. I'm fairly certain I'll die if you don't say yes." Her words were almost a chant and there was no way Dex could answer her because he was fighting his own demons. The little devil on his shoulder who catered to his selfish side was shouting that he should take what he wanted...*it's right there in front of you...take it...it's yours*. Luckily for Mary, his inner Dom was more in control, at least for the moment.

Dex felt Ash shift her up slightly, then her scream rent the air around them as Ash pushed inside in one long glide. They'd attracted a small crowd but he was sure Mary was beyond noticing. "Fuck that feels so good. If I died this instant, you all could tell my family I went to meet my maker a happy man. Pet, we're going to start moving and I want you to hold off just as long as you can. The longer you wait the better it will be.

"Oh God. Surely it can't get any better than this."

Oh, sweetheart, you have no idea. You're going to see angels strumming their harps it's going to feel so good. They set up an alternating rhythm—when Dex pulled back Ash pushed in, over and over again until the room started to spin around them. Mary began moaning as her entire body trembled and quaked. Dex hoped his knees wouldn't give out because his vision was already starting to blur at the intensity of the pleasure racking his body like pounding waves.

During their earlier negotiations for this scene, Mary had mentioned her work schedule was going to become particularly intense for a few weeks, and he'd gotten the impression she wanted to try a ménage scene before work began taking over her club time. The public play part of their planned scene had been a much tougher sell, but she'd finally agreed at least to try. He simply couldn't imagine not repeating this because it was probably going down as the most pleasurable experience of his life. Feeling his partner's cock sliding along the thin membrane separating them was also ratcheting up the intensity and, for the first time since he'd first shared a woman, he was already thinking about their next encounter.

Before Mary, neither Dex nor Ash had played with the same sub more than twice—hell, they didn't usually take the same sub more than once. They had made a single exception before they'd met the beautiful woman between them and were still dealing with the disastrous consequences. They were also still dodging that woman at the club. The simple truth was Trish Jantz was attractive enough but she wasn't a true submissive. She played the game, but her submission was an act rather than the core of her personality as it was with Mary.

No, there was no way he and Ash could give this up. Sharing Mary in the most intimate way possible had forged a bond between the three of them the instant he and Ash had both sunk into her sweet body at the same time. Returning his focus to the writhing woman in front of him, Dex promised himself they'd make it so incredible for her she wouldn't be able to stay away. And if she did—they'd go to her, because there was no way he was waiting weeks to enjoy this again.

Leaning down, Dex opened his mouth over the soft curve of her shoulder, once again dragging his teeth along the peak until he settled along the curved junction where her shoulder met her neck. Biting down harder this time, he was stunned at the speed and intensity of her reaction. Her response to that small bit of control and pain was textbook perfect. Mary's muscles locked down in a powerful squeeze that swept the last remnants of control right out from under him. Somewhere in the back of his mind, Dex registered her scream of release and Ash's groan just before he felt his friend pulse on the other side of the thin membrane separating them. By the time Dex's vision cleared, he and Ash were both clinging to the chains holding the rope chair Mary was still secured in. They were no longer holding it to keep it from swaying wildly, their white-knuckled grips were the only thing keeping them on their feet.

When Dex finally managed to suck in enough oxygen to bring his muddled brain back on-line, he pulled out of Mary's quivering ass. When she moaned at the loss, he stroked his hand soothingly up and down her spine until she settled. He and Ash both cleaned themselves up quickly and then set about caring for Mary. He couldn't wait to set up their next scene and four weeks wasn't even an option.

Chapter One

ASH MOORE GLARED at his best friend, Dex Raines, as they watched the elderly doctor who'd been closing the gash on Ash's arm tie off the last stitch. The man had to be eighty or more, but the gleam of mischief in his eyes was easy to see as he leaned back to admire his work. "How'd you say you did this again?" Ash knew the old fart was just torturing him, hell, the man was probably old enough to be his grandfather, but was obviously sharp as a tack despite the fact he'd asked Ash to repeat the story no less than three times since they'd arrived. Doc Davis hadn't missed anything happening around him the entire time Ash and Dex had been in the small hospital's emergency room, so it was clear he was just fucking with Ash. Hell, the man had barked out orders to nurses attending various patients without ever looking up from his work as he neatly stitched his arm.

Ash took a calming breath before reluctantly answering—again, "Skateboarding."

"With the bosses' wife...don't forget that part." Dex wasn't making any effort to hide his amusement, completely ignoring his best friend's glower.

Honestly, as long as we've been friends, you would think the prick would know better than to jack with me when I haven't gotten laid in...fucking weeks.

"Tobi challenged him and Lord knows Mr. Intimidating here can't let a challenge from a tiny, blond tornado go unanswered. So now, Tobi is back upstairs at Prairie Winds tending to her babies, and Ash gets to spend the afternoon here with you." By the time Dex finished, he was laughing out loud and the doctor who'd been trying valiantly to play the straight man finally let a grin spread over his wrinkled face and chuckled.

"That woman is a menace. Jesus, I'd sooner deal with a bunch of religious extremists—at least you know what those bastards are about." *Yep, they're all trying to get into their version of heaven and chase virgins. Newsflash, dip-shits...if they were old enough to die virgins, there's a fucking reason—they're all butt-fuck ugly or mean as snakes.* "No, I've got to be terrorized by a five foot nothing blond Tasmanian Devil in Prada. What the hell were Kent and Kyle thinking marrying her?" Everybody, including Ash, knew his words were hollow. He had a soft spot for Tobi West the size of the Grand Canyon and everyone, including Tobi, knew it. The little imp had played Ash like a song as her husbands had stood aside shaking their heads at his naïveté.

The doctor's eyes lit up even more, merriment dancing in their cobalt depths at the mention of Tobi's name. His gaze slid from Ash to Dex, "Tobi? Tobi West?" When Dex nodded, the doctor laughed out loud, "Oh, she's a firecracker, that one. Lordy but that girl reminds me of Lilly at that age. Those men of hers have their hands full I'm tellin' ya, and I don't think I've ever known two fellas that deserve the grief more. Hell, I think those West boys' frequent emergency room visits kept this place in the black for years." The man was still chuckling as he shuffled out of the room. Ash shook his head and smiled despite his humiliation.

"It didn't really need stitches, you know. It was just a

scratch," Ash grumbled as Dex tossed him the tattered shirt he'd been wearing earlier. Ash easily snagged the shirt out of the air and frowned. The black t-shirt he was still wearing had survived his crash better than the button-down oxford his mom had given him last year for his birthday. *Maybe if I roll up the sleeves I won't look like some homeless person off the street. Hopefully Mom has replacement wardrobe items on this year's list.*

"The doctor just put *twelve* stitches in your arm, Superman. Get your cape on so we can get out of here." Ash knew Dex disliked hospitals as much as he did, and Dex was probably more than ready to get out of this one. When you're a soldier, and particularly when you are a member of the Special Forces, you only go into hospitals under extreme circumstances, and twelve lousy stitches in his arm didn't qualify. Hell, the whole incident was fucking humiliating if the truth was to be known. A skateboarding accident? Christ, he'd survived missions to every hellhole in the world without so much as a scratch—*well, maybe a few minor dings here and there*—but to end up in the emergency room because he'd fallen off a kid's toy was just plain embarrassing. Not to mention Tobi West was never going to let him hear the end of it. *Christ, who am I kidding, nobody at the club is going to forget this in a year full of Sundays.*

Stepping out of the small treatment room, Ash instinctively scanned the corridor. He and Dex had only been officially retired for a few weeks, and he hadn't fully decompressed yet. A part of him knew he'd never be completely free of the cautionary habits BUD/S and his years as a SEAL had drilled into him—they were just second nature now. Relaxing when he realized there weren't any people in their immediate vicinity, a small group at the far end of the hall caught his eye. *Something familiar...* There were only three people—two men in tailored suits flanking a woman in a pale aqua business suit that hugged her body like a second skin. Her hourglass figure was perfect and the sway of her hips in the stilettos she was wearing was enough to send a man into a hypnotic stupor. When he raised his eyes, he realized she had hair exactly the same color as Mary Dillon. *What the fuck?*

Ash and Dex had been at the Prairie Winds Club the night Mary and her hateful friend, Kelly Mason, had cornered Tobi in the ladies' lounge and slung every bit of verbal trash at her they could dig up. After sorting it all out, it had been clear Kelly had been the instigator and Mary's culpability in the entire mess was her poor choice of friends. Everyone who'd listened to the story believed Mary had been trying to appease her new friend even though she didn't have any personal feelings toward Tobi one way or another. Kelly's motivation had been simple enough to figure out, she'd wanted to eliminate a competitor for the West brothers' attention. The viper had joined the club for the sole purpose of meeting Kyle and Kent West. Both men had tried on several occasions to politely deter Kelly, but she'd been relentless in her advances toward them both.

Kelly and Mary's actions had come to light when club member, Noelle Chambers, heard their harsh words and intervened. Noelle might be submissive to her husband, Neal, but she is also a successful prosecutor in Austin, and her take no prisoners approach that night had put both women in the hot seat in a big hurry. Noelle had escorted a traumatized Tobi out to the Wests before returning to the lounge. No one had actually witnessed what had occurred behind that closed door, but Kelly had stormed out spitting mad and threatening to call the police to have Noelle charged with assault. Everyone within hearing distance had burst out laughing because it was absurd to even entertain the idea any law enforcement officer would arrest a prosecutor for doing something no one had seen, and everyone else would have done.

In the end, Kelly had refused to accept responsibility for her actions or the punishment that would follow. She'd been banned from the Prairie Winds Club for life and her name had been forwarded to every other club in their extensive network as well. Not that anyone thought the spoiled rich girl had a sincere interest in the lifestyle, but Ash doubted she liked being excluded from anything either.

Mary Dillon had tearfully confessed her part and her sincere apology and obvious remorse had saved her club membership, contingent upon a punishment of Dex and Ash's choosing and a suspension. Their punishment had been harsh, but it had quickly become obvious the young woman was not adverse to the pain—in fact she'd relished it. She'd quickly slipped in to sub-space and they'd had to pull her back from the edge of orgasm several times. Ash considered himself a borderline sadist, despite most of his friends' disagreement with the assessment. The euphoria he experienced when he was able to push a sub just to that nanosecond before she broke was pure ambrosia for him. And even though Dex didn't find the adrenaline rush Ash did in walking that fine line between pushing a sub's limits to the max and going over the top, he was still a Master in administering just the right amount of pain to willing subs to launch them into Nirvana.

During Mary's very public punishment that night, it had been clear she hadn't been trained properly and by the time they'd finished, Ash had been more than a little worried about her lack of boundaries. The woman had a pain tolerance level that rivaled the best Special Forces soldiers he'd ever known. More than once during the scene Ash had deliberately pushed her, hoping to prompt her to recognize or at least question her limits, but she'd failed to even call "yellow" let alone letting the safe-word out. A submissive without clear boundaries was a danger to herself and to her Dom. Ash and Dex had played with Mary several times since that night, and they'd tried to teach her the importance of recognizing and enforcing her limits. Neither of them was convinced they'd succeeded yet—it was an on-going process.

Since that night they had played exclusively with Mary. They'd both lost interest in any of the other subs they'd shared before they'd met her. They had also seen her a few times in social situations, but those had always involved Masters and subs from the club so their opportunities to get to know each other had been somewhat limited. While Regi had been gone recently, Mary had filled in occasionally, and Ash had heard both Kent and Kyle raving about her organizational skills.

When the deplorable conditions Regi, the club's business manager and "go to girl", had been living in came to light, Ash and Dex had met with Kyle to check on Mary. They'd been worried she might be suffering the same fate, but Kyle had assured them they didn't need to worry. Oddly enough, Kyle's awkward attempts to placate them had only made them more curious. Dex had agreed with Ash's observation, Kyle had danced around the answers in a way that was completely out of character for the team leader they'd known, and his evasiveness had only raised more questions.

Ash and Dex both understood the importance of maintaining confidentiality relating to the club members lives outside of the club, and they'd followed Kyle's suggestion to ask Mary directly. Thinking back on how *that* had played out, he could only shake his head in exasperation, hell, he still couldn't believe how easily she had just flat outmaneuvered them during the conversation. Dex had let Ash take the lead because, in general, people were much more intimidated by him. Mary had answered each question despite her obvious reluctance, but it had been clear she was choosing her words carefully and he'd known she wasn't being completely forthcoming. The only thing that had kept him from pursuing the subject was the fact he'd also known she wasn't lying when she'd insisted they didn't have any reason to be concerned and that she was indeed "living in a safe place with adequate provisions."

He felt Dex freeze beside him and Ash knew he was watching the woman as well. "Who is that?" Leave it to Dex to cut straight to the chase.

"No clue, but there is something familiar about her—the way she moves, but I can't believe I would have forgotten her." When the younger man on her right put his hand on her back as they approached the elevator, Ash felt himself stiffen. *What the hell is wrong with me? I don't even know her, and I certainly don't have any claim to her.* He heard the low growl in the back of Dex's throat and wondered if his partner was having the same reaction to the intimacy of the touch. The man's hand was higher than a Dom would have touched her, but the familiarity and affection in his eyes was easy to see when he'd turned toward them. Ash had the distinct impression the man and woman they were watching were together but not a couple, and the man on her left was some sort of hospital whosy-who. When she turned to the open elevator doors, Ash felt his mouth fall open and he heard Dex softy mutter, "What the fuck?"

Ash had only caught the briefest look at her profile, but heard the faint sound of her laughter at something the older man had said. He'd caught just a couple of her words before she'd disappeared into the elevator, but he'd recognized the light sound of her voice immediately. He was ashamed to admit he hadn't even realized they'd never heard Mary laugh until several months after they'd met. It had only dawned on him when he'd heard her laugh at something Tobi had said while the two of them had been settled on the loungers by the pool. Mary's laugh wasn't a girlish giggle, it was full, resonate, and it had made him smile. After that day, Ash had made it his personal mission to hear the sound as often as possible, but today when he'd heard it, everything in him had stilled.

Hearing Dex's snarled, "Who the fuck has his hands on her and why didn't we know she was attached to another man?" Ash could only stare numbly at the elevator doors as they slid closed. Out of the corner of his eye he saw Dex stop a young nurse that had been passing by. Through the fog clouding his mind, he registered Dex's inquiry, "Excuse me, can you tell me who the people were that just got on the elevator and where they might be heading? The woman looked like a friend of ours, but neither of us got a good look at her."

Ash had always admired Dex's ability to use his looks to charm even the most resistant woman, and the petite brunette whose nametag read "Carla S., R.N." didn't appear to be immune to what the other members of their SEAL team had called the "Dex Effect" than any other woman Ash had ever met. It didn't seem to matter if they were eight or eighty; women genuinely liked Dex Raines. Her eyes glazed over a little looking up into Dex's blue eyes, and she gave them a breathy run-down, "The older man is Mr. Adler, he's the head of the hospital's board of directors. The pretty lady in the middle is Merilee D. Lanham, she heads up the Lanham Foundation, and the other man is her assistant, Tony Ballard."

"Thank you, Carla. You've been very helpful." Ash looked away to suppress his grin when he noticed Dex's hand had gently shackled the sweet nurse's wrist and his thumb was drawing lazy circles along the inside over her pulse point. Biting back his own words, Ash waited for Dex to find out where the trio had been headed. "Darlin', do you by any chance know where they were headed? We'd like to catch up with Ms. Lanham." *And isn't that the understatement of the year?*

After learning the group was heading to the hospital's outdoor courtyard for a media event—*whatever the fuck that meant*—to announce plans for a new women's and children's care wing, he and Dex made their way down the stairs. They followed the throng of people headed that way, many of whom were speculating about rumors the new wing was going to be named after the two newest physicians on staff. Ash didn't understand the significance of those concerns, but it was evidently hot news among those making their way into the crowded courtyard. They passed a sign at the entrance that proclaimed Ms. Merilee D. Lanham, CEO of the Lanham Foundation, would be today's special guest. *Why had she told them her name was Mary? Wait. Had she told them? Or had someone else?* Hell, his brain was so scrambled at the moment he could barely remember the details that had just been rolling through his mind a few minutes earlier. But now that he thought back on that night, he was fairly certain it had been Kyle who referred to her as Mary Dillon.

Concentrating on that memory as they made their way

inside the courtyard, he remembered thinking Kyle had stumbled over her name because it hadn't sounded quite right when he'd pronounced it. Had Kyle actually said *Meri* and he and Dex had merely assumed he'd said Mary? Shaking off his wayward thoughts, Ash watched Merilee D. Lanham schmooze with dignitaries and staff members at the front of the enclosed area. She looked completely relaxed and at ease surrounded by all the suits. A brilliant smile they'd seen far too rarely lit up her face, making her glow from the inside out. He'd known she was attractive, but with her long dark hair framing her tan face then falling in soft waves over her shoulders to the middle of her back, he realized she was heart-stoppingly beautiful. Even from this distance, he could see her bright green eyes sparkling with life as she effortlessly moved between the people vying for her attention.

They stayed at the back, choosing to forego the seating that had been set up facing a small raised flowerbed at one end of the enclosed garden area. A clear lectern held a microphone on the wide step surrounding the oval bed providing a colorful background for whoever would be speaking. Standing in the shadows close to the rock wall of the hospital, they'd be able to see the speaker without being easy to spot.

"For some reason I'm pissed. And the hell of it is, I'm not even sure why." Dex's comment echoed Ash's own frustration. Even after he'd learned the man touching Mary was her assistant, Ash could still feel the residual effects of the sudden surge of jealousy that had swamped him—he didn't understand it and he damned well didn't like it. He'd played in various clubs all over the world never thinking twice about the scenes being anything more than consenting adults engaging in an activity that was *hopefully* mutually gratifying. He and Dex had always been absolutely candid with the subs they'd spent time with, explaining clearly there were no commitments involved. And all but a very few had not only understood but been of like minds.

Ash watched the group of people at the sidelines and was surprised to see Regi standing next to Mary. Nodding in her direction, Ash asked, "What do you suppose Regi is doing here? She seems more than a little uncomfortable." Regi and uncomfortable just didn't go together, that alone had him wondering where her men were just as the two OB-GYNs walked up beside her. Both men greeted Mary with obvious affection, but their attention was clearly centered on their fiancée. Ash had been at the party where Regi agreed to marry the docs, but as far as he knew, the trio hadn't gotten around to setting a date yet. So much had changed in the little imp's life in such a short period of time, her discomfort wasn't all that difficult to understand. The mystery was how the two women knew each other outside Prairie Winds.

Chapter Two

W HEN THE MAN Nurse Carla S. had indicated was the president of the regional medical center's board stepped up to the podium, everyone fell silent. Dex Raines listened as Mr. Full-of-Himself droned on about the "needs" of the community and while Dex appreciated that his points were likely valid, the man's hard-sell approach was grating on his last nerve. Leaning close to Ash, he whispered, "Whatcha bet he was a car salesman?" Ash's snort of laughter earned them glares from several people standing nearby, but the amusement in their eyes had belied the scornful expressions. The man continued yammering away until Dex felt his eyelids start to slide south. Christ he'd gone days without sleep on missions without breaking a sweat, and here he was, about to fall into a stupor standing up. "I think I've just discovered the cure for insomnia." More shushing came from the peanut gallery but this time Ash hadn't been the only one fighting to hold back his laughter.

Dex listened as the man finally introduced Merilee, he watched as she graciously shook Mr. Sure-Doze's hand before stepping behind the clear podium. She thanked everyone for taking time to attend and Dex was impressed with her ability to engage the audience. Taking a quick scan of the courtyard, he noticed everyone in the audience seemed to be as enthralled with her as he was. It was clear she was at ease speaking in front of groups, and the woman standing on the makeshift stage was one hundred eighty degrees out from the sub he knew from the club. *Fuck me! That is exactly why she…like so many others, has to keep her public and private lives distinctly compartmentalized.* Merilee D. Lanham's public persona and success would depend upon her private lifestyle choices remaining private…*very, very private.* It didn't take a rocket scientist to figure out how devastating it would be to her career, and to the charitable foundation she headed, if word got out that she edged toward masochism and frequented the city's hottest kink club.

Merilee Lanham was clearly a force to be reckoned with outside of the bedroom and for the briefest moment, Dex wondered if he and Ash would be able to handle those two very distinct personalities. He'd heard Neal Chambers talking to Dean and Dell West about the challenges he and Noelle faced trying to reconcile their "public faces" with their private lifestyle. Neal was a popular pediatrician who was quickly making a name for himself not only in Texas, but also nationally, and Noelle's position as a tough-as-nails-prosecutor was garnering her a lot of political attention as well. Since Lilly West's charity work kept her in the public eye, Dean and Dell understood the young physician's concerns and had offered him several bits of advice that Dex wished now he had listened to more carefully.

In Dex's mind, he'd already started thinking of the woman holding the audience in the palm of her hand as Merilee, because she clearly wasn't the shy submissive they'd been drawn to at the club. And even though he wasn't sure he or Ash would ever fit in to her world, his respect for her—and the work she was doing—was growing with every word she spoke. She was obviously passionate about the care of women and children, and excited to announce the Lanham Foundation was partnering with another donor to fund the lion's share of the new wing. Both Dex and Ash had joined the others in their thunderous applause when Regi's part in the project was announced.

They'd been along when Regi had "rediscovered" the sunken treasure her parents had been salvaging when her dad's double life had finally caught up with him. The Prairie Winds team's entire operation had been FUBAR almost from the beginning, but had really become fucked up beyond all recognition a few weeks ago when Regi swore she'd seen her dad on a boat anchored in the river behind the club. Hell, if she had, then Mark Stephano had just "survived" his second "death" and Dex was starting to think he might be some sort of magician instead of the CIA spook he'd once been. *Jesus, Joseph, and Mary...I was sure no one could have survived that mess.* The sunken ship had been perched precariously on the edge of a deep underwater ridge and when everything had finally shifted enough to tip the balance, Stephano and several of his men had been pulled over the edge to their deaths by the sheer force of the water's movement—or so they'd all thought.

Dex had been impressed as hell with Regi while they'd been in Belize. When she'd first arrived, Regi had learned her longtime friend and mentor had died. The news had shaken her to be sure, but she'd sucked it up and driven herself to the point of exhaustion because she hadn't wanted to burden the other members of the team. And now, Regi's decision to use a huge percentage of the money, from the sale of the artifacts they'd recovered, to help build a facility designed to serve the local community endeared her to Dex even more. Dex smiled when he saw

Regi's future husbands standing to the side watching her, pride easy to see in their eyes. Both Kirk Evans and Brian Bennett had the same sappy grin Dex has seen on the faces of the other Doms at Prairie Winds when they'd found the woman that completed them.

For the first time Dex could remember, he actually found himself wondering what it would be like to *know* you'd found the woman fate had sent you. Ash often teased him about his "new age" ideas, but it had never changed Dex's view. There was a universal truth and comforting peace found in the knowledge there are forces larger than any one individual that Dex believed was undeniable, and he knew Ash would see it too—when the time was right.

THE HAIR ON the back of Meri's neck stood straight up just as she was stepping into the hospital's elevator and she wasn't even sure what had set her senses on alert. But whatever it was, the feeling had been unsettling and she was still feeling the effects even now. She wanted to chalk it up to the fact she'd been experiencing a significant increase in security challenges recently but hadn't yet taken her dad's advice and hired personal protection...but that didn't feel quite right. *Probably ought to be reconsidering that decision Ms. Harvard MBA.*

Meri had planned to speak with Jax and Micah about updating the security system at her home, but she hadn't been able to catch them alone at the club. The last thing she'd wanted was for Dex Raines or Ash Moore to get wind of the trouble she was having. She'd seen the other former SEALs at the club in "over-protective mode" and it wasn't pretty...heck, it was downright oppressive. And it wasn't as if she actually *belonged* to Dex and Ash, they hadn't acted the least bit interested in having a relationship outside of the club. Even that wouldn't likely change the fact they'd happily take the opportunity to punish her for not telling them about the recent trouble she'd been experiencing. Cripes, now that she thought about it, Kyle and Kent were probably going to go postal as well. Sighing to herself, she resolved to call Kent today on her way home, he was usually the most reasonable of the club's brood of mother hens.

Jax and Micah had been busy with Gracie and their new daughter. Their wife, Gracie, had a difficult pregnancy and little Miss Deaga Drake-McDonald hadn't opted for a peaceful entry in to her parents' life on any level, and from what Meri had heard, the little dark haired beauty was still giving them a run for their money. She dreaded adding to Micah and Jax's burdens, but she had a sinking feeling her choices in the matter were narrowing quickly.

Quite frankly, she was more than a little impressed Parker Andrews hadn't already sung like a proverbial canary. Parker had worked for the Austin Police Department but he'd recently taken a special investigator position at the Texas Rangers state office in Austin. Meri's family was well connected politically, so a couple of agents from the Ranger's office had shown up after the most recent break-in. *It won't matter the incident should be considered confidential.* Meri knew good Doms considered it their responsibility to protect submissives—in fact, most of what she'd read said it was their highest calling. *Crapamolie, it's just a matter of time before this whole fiasco blows up in my face.*

Waiting for the hospital's board president to finish his spiel, Meri tried to surreptitiously scan the courtyard. There were more people in attendance than she had anticipated, so obviously someone had gotten the word out, and that worked well for the ambitious plan they were setting into motion today. In truth, she'd been working on this project for almost a year, with her vision for expanded services only now becoming public. And while she believed in what she was doing, there was still a small part of her that worried her ex-boyfriend was simply waiting in the dark shadows surrounding the courtyard ready to pounce. There was something in the air...some underlying energy edged with danger lurking at the fringes of the crowd, but Meri wasn't having any luck identifying the source. John Stevens' threats to expose her as a slut with a predilection for pain scared her far more than she'd let anyone know. If he was behind her recent rash of trouble, she knew he would be very hard to catch. He wasn't extremely wealthy, but he was very well connected and highly motivated to discredit her.

Every lash of John Stevens' tongue had left a ragged scar on her soul. Some were small...others were enormous, but each one had left an indelible mark and eroded her self-confidence. Despite what others might see, Merilee Dillon Lanham was still a woman with all the same insecurities other women faced. John's scathing comments about her appearance had cut her to the core, she still heard them echoing through her mind every time she looked in the mirror. It didn't matter that she came from an incredibly privileged background or that most women would have been envious of her appearance. When Meri looked in the mirror, the first thing she saw was each of her flaws.

She'd been more than a little worried the pompous ass would use today's press gathering to his advantage. When she'd learned his staff had forwarded his regrets, she'd breathed a sigh of uneasy relief. What she had been too ashamed to share with anyone was the fact her ex had been emotionally abusive almost from the beginning, and his behavior had quickly escalated to the point she'd become fearful for her safety.

Once she'd started researching domestic abuse, she'd immediately recognized the pattern of behavior the books had described. It had begun with complaints about everything—he found fault with anything and everything she did or said. Nothing she did was or ever would have been good enough. There had been several nights that he'd screamed at her for so long he had actually gone hoarse. But it was Senator John Stevens' threats to destroy her reputation that resonated the loudest in her mind. His vicious verbal attacks resounded loud and clear anytime she scheduled a press conference. Just thinking about a reporter asking her about her fondness for pain or her membership to one of the most popular BDSM clubs in the state sent shards of icy-fear through her. She wasn't sure who would be damaged the most in the media frenzy that would ensue, likely they'd both sink like the Titanic.

Somewhere along the way John had decided her interest in BDSM was an affront to his sexual prowess, which really was laughable when she considered they'd only had sex a handful of times. *No reason to repeat any of those ninety-second wonders.* Why had she trusted him when every instinct she possessed had warned her he was a predator? Why had she let this man slip through when she should have known he was like every other man who had ever pursued her? Men were only interested in her for one reason—her parents' money and political influence. And how on earth had he convinced her to reveal what she needed most in the bedroom?

Shaking off the memory of how that last night with John had shattered all of her dreams, Meri refocused her attention to the task at hand. *Good God in heaven above, surely Mr. Bluster is getting close to finished.* When he finally introduced her, Meri stepped behind the podium and instinct took over, allowing her to move easily through her prepared remarks. Her memory had always been phenomenal. From the time she'd been able to talk, her parents and teachers had marveled at her ability to recall even the minutest detail of something she'd seen or heard. She'd been tested numerous times in school and the last she'd heard the psychologists were still arguing whether her memory was eidetic or photographic. Personally she'd never cared—it was useful and that was all that mattered to her. *After all, just because I can remember minutia doesn't make me smart…and it damned well didn't make me a good judge of character when I got involved with John.*

The audience was reacting just as she'd hoped they would and all the right media outlets were in attendance, but something was still *off* although she was too distracted at the moment to sort it out. Continuing to feed the group's enthusiasm with the architect's rendered drawings, she could almost feel the enthusiasm of the group growing. The entire project was going to require a tremendous amount of community support in addition to the Lanham Foundation's seed money and Regi's generous donation, so today's announcement was also the unofficial kick-off for the fundraising effort. She'd been happy to see many of the wealthier locals in attendance, but less than thrilled to see Kelly Mason was among them.

Meri had attended very exclusive schools so she hadn't met Kelly until they'd both become members of Prairie Winds at the same time. She'd found out later their parents had known each other for years, and that her dad had gone to considerable effort to ensure she and Kelly's paths didn't cross. She'd confided in her mother after the incident at Prairie Winds...well, she hadn't really had any choice when her mom had walked into the dressing room while they'd been shopping and seen the bruises from her punishment. *Oh yeah, that had been an interesting moment. Crap on a cracker, I didn't think she was ever going to stop sobbing.*

She wasn't sure exactly what her mom had told her father, but she was convinced it was a heavily diluted version of the truth. She'd never known her mother to lie, but she was an Olympic champion at spin. Meri had often thought her mom missed her calling, she should have been a political speechwriter...hell, the woman could make Judas look like a victim. Later that evening, her dad swirled his wine around in the heavy crystal goblet he held and looked at her thoughtfully for several torturous moments before tactfully cautioning her to guard her privacy and to avoid "that Mason tramp" at all costs. In the months that followed, Meri had noted the foundation had quietly pulled out of several projects they'd been working on in conjunction with Kelly's family.

Meri knew he was smoothing the way before she actually assumed complete control of the foundation and appreciated his efforts. Even though she was already the CEO, her dad was still the Chairman of the Board, and she relied heavily on his experience while earning her own. Thinking about her parents made her smile. They never did anything by half measure—they lived in the moment and each of those to the fullest. They were currently on a "cultural excursion" in Peru. Her mother had always been interested in the history and cultures of the people of Central and South America, so Meri hadn't been surprised when she'd persuaded her doting husband to travel high into the Andes to explore the history of the Incas.

She'd been happy to hand the microphone over to the next speaker, but she heard him re-introduce her so she pulled her thoughts back to the moment and smiled as she once again took center stage. They'd set aside a few minutes for photos and questions, but looking out over the sea of reporters, Meri had a sudden urge to bolt. There was an undercurrent of strange energy coursing through the group and she felt a shiver of anxiety work its way up her spine. She had always prided herself on her ability to judge people…or she had before dating John and befriending Kelly, now she wasn't as sure of herself in that regard. It was that unease that had kept her from revealing her real name to Ash Moore and Dex Raines. *Holy mother of God…just thinking about them makes my body sit up and take notice.*

As if her desire alone had wished them into existence, Meri caught the briefest glimpse of Dex standing in the dark shadows at her left. Her breath caught at the sight, and his stance was so confident, yet pulsing with questions. His feet were shoulder width apart, arms crossed over his broad chest, his head tipped ever so slightly to the side as if he was studying her. *Oh, you can bet your sweet—soon to be very sore ass—he's studying you, Merilee. Did you think he or Ash would be happy to find out the sub they've been playing with isn't who they assumed she was?* Although she had never actually lied to them, she hadn't been particularly generous with information either. Sighing to herself in resignation, she glanced again and saw Ash had moved up alongside Dex. *Wait…what happened to his arm?* As if he'd read her mind, she saw his head shake ever so slightly as if telling her to not be concerned about something he considered inconsequential, but damn it, his arm was bandaged from his elbow to just above his wrist.

Seeing the two of them poised along the side of the courtyard's open area explained the strange movement she'd sensed in the crowd a few minutes earlier. Like rippling waves in water, people had stepped forward and then back, now she knew they'd been making way for the two large men to pass behind them. *How long have they been here?* Thinking about them watching her speak to the group gripped her with a mixture of pride in the way she'd held everyone's attention and anxiety about how they might view the real Meri.

She'd known from the beginning they'd assumed her name was Mary simply by the way they'd pronounced it. She hadn't bothered to correct them because if nothing else, her sweet southern mama had drilled manners deep into her very being. *It's not nice to tell others they are incompetent, even if they are Merilee. And it's good to be smarter than the people around, but you start calling attention to it and they'll turn mean as snakes in the time it takes you to blink.* It had been wonderful advice, but this was one of the few times she'd actually considered she was going to seriously regret listening to her mama.

Answering most of the reporters' questions had been easy because the vast majority of them had been anticipated, so she and the others easily rattled off their previously prepared answers. But when the skinny guy with the cheap toupee she'd seen Kelly talking to earlier held up his hand, Meri felt a quick sweep of fear at the knowing smirk on his face. "Ms. Lanham, our readers have been asking about your recent break-up with Senator Stevens. Can you tell us what happened between the two of you? And whether or not it was the result of a particular social affiliation?" Her mind was reeling and she knew her deer in the headlights look gave away her surprise. *Recent? Is he kidding? We broke up almost a year ago! Social affiliation? He knows about my membership at the club?*

Once her brain finally re-engaged, she gave him the smile every southern woman knows how to wield ruthless-ly...the one that said, *I'm going to kill you with kindness as I mow you down at the ankles with words you'll spend days trying to unravel.* "Well, it's unfortunate you seem to have been given some awfully old news. You are asking about something that happened almost a year ago and is not even remotely connected to the reason we're here. I'd hate to waste everyone's time with something no one cares anything about. If you'll call my office I'll be *happy* to speak with you about your concerns." Okay, *happy* was a total lie and everyone knew it, but she wasn't going to play his game with cameras rolling all around her. Just as the jackass started to open his mouth again, she saw his eyes widen as they shifted to her left. It didn't take her long to figure out why. Ash and Dex had positioned themselves at the side of the makeshift stage. Their mirrored stances making their intent clear, and if she hadn't known better, she would have jumped to the same conclusion she was sure everyone else had, they were a part of her personal protection team. In fact she had often used security services when she was traveling and had hoped to talk with Micah and Jax about providing those services in the future, but she'd hesitated fearing club gossip would eventually catch up with her. *Well, doesn't look like that particular excuse is necessary now...damn and double damn.*

Chapter Three

D EX HAD GONE on alert when he'd spotted Kelly Mason standing off to the side watching Meri with narrowed eyes. The woman was a straight up bitch in his opinion, and her body language fairly well shouted her disdain for Merilee Lanham. The instant the scrawny prick Dex had seen the demon-woman talking to earlier got to his feet, the hair on the back of his neck stood up as if a wave of static electricity had rolled over him. He growled, "Let's go" under his breath and started moving forward knowing Ash was right behind him. Dex was grateful he and Ash had already moved closer to the small makeshift stage during the first part of the question and answer portion of the program. They hadn't anticipated trouble, they had simply not wanted *Ms. Lanham* to slip away before they had a chance to speak with her. *Oh yeah, sweet cheeks, we are definitely going to have a nice long chat about transparency and the fact that lying by omission is the same as flat-out deception.*

The reporter's question had rattled Meri, but Dex had been damned impressed with how quickly she'd recovered. He also wanted to howl with laughter at the icy response the little prick had definitely deserved. *If that boy isn't from the south, he probably doesn't know he's just been filleted with a smile.* Dex hadn't been raised in Texas, but he would have recognized that smile a mile away. He'd been gifted with the same expression by his sweet mama back in Georgia on more than one occasion. And even though both of his older sisters had left the South, they hadn't lost their ability to flash that same smile—*seems once a genteel lady learns that particular lesson, they keep it.*

Since Ash hadn't questioned him, Dex was sure he had also noticed Kelly Mason chatting up the little prick who had just sent a flash of pink into the perfectly tanned cheeks of Ms. Lanham. A quick glance to his side confirmed his suspicions. The lines of strain around his friend's eyes and mouth told Dex just how close Ash was to grabbing Mr. Nosey-Reporter up by the scruff of his neck and escorting him into a nice secluded alley to chat. They had both worked personal security for Jax and Micah a few times, so it was easy to assume that don't-fuck-with-me posture when they'd stopped a few feet to Meri's left. She hadn't seen them approach—another thing they'd be talking to her about—until she noticed the change in the reporter's expression.

"If he so much as flinches I'm snatching him up by his short and curlies…what a piss-ant." Dex had to hold back his smile at Ash's threat, it wasn't that he considered it empty, because Dex had known Ash Moore since they'd both been pea-green recruits, and knew what his friend was capable of. They'd gone through Basic Training and BUD/S together, discovering they had actually grown up just a few miles apart. The fact they hadn't met until they were adults was likely a godsend considering what a holy terror Dex had been. They'd bonded quickly and considered themselves brothers in every sense of the word except blood. Dex doubted there would ever be a situation where he couldn't predict within a microsecond how and when Ash was going to react. No, Ash's threat was amusing because it was just exactly what he'd been thinking himself.

Yes, indeed...battered and bruised would be a nice look for the little twerp.

Thankfully the hospital's CFO managed to pull himself away from Meri's assistant long enough to step forward and politely thank everyone for coming. His words essentially ended the informal question-answer portion of the gathering. Even though he was grateful, Dex wanted to shake both men for being so distracted they hadn't managed to look out after the guest of honor. The financial officer seemed to be completely infatuated by Mr. Best Dressed Look-at-me Tony Ballard. Fuck it, both of them were the kind of men that made every woman they passed do a double take. It stood to reason they had to be reasonably intelligent, but Dex was betting both men struggled to keep their personal lives on an even keel. Dex recognized the barely contained hunger in the two men's eyes, still—he vowed to remind Mr. Ballard that a large part of his job as Merilee's assistant revolved around keeping his lovely boss safe.

While the pretty-boy CFO encouraged members of the audience to watch for further announcements and updates, Dex wanted nothing more than to lead Ms. Lanham through the crowd and right out to his truck. But he stood quietly beside Ash and watched—everything. His eyes continually scanning the area for possible threats. Old habits weren't always worth breaking and he couldn't shake the feeling there was more than one threat milling close. Even though he didn't get the impression the reporter who'd questioned her about her ex was a threat in a physical sense, he could certainly hurt her professionally. Dex knew enough about women to know the fall-out of having her *kinks* exposed would be emotionally devastating, and that was what worried him the most, he'd always sensed a vulnerability in Meri. She was a borderline masochist who didn't have a strong enough sense of self-preservation in Dex's opinion. But even more significant was the fact she was also a submissive who would always see herself in whatever she saw reflected in her Master's eyes, so she could easily let things go too far seeking his approval.

Merilee Lanham's pleasure during a scene was so closely linked to pain, Dex wondered if she'd be able to orgasm without it. *That is something we need to work on.* But outside of that specific dynamic, she was a "pleaser" of the highest order. Her happiness was dependent upon making the other people in her life happy. If she belonged to them, Dex knew for certain one of their biggest challenges would be teaching her to recognize and respect her own limits. He doubted the woman ever said no to anyone—hell, she'd probably run herself into the ground helping others if they didn't monitor her closely. *Oh, Ash and I will definitely stop that nonsense in short order.*

They gave her a few minutes to say her good byes and as soon as they saw her assistant moving toward Meri, they both stepped forward flanking her. Their synchronized movement made it look as if they'd rehearsed it and Dex had to hold back his smile at the impressed expressions on the faces surrounding them. *If they only knew how many times we really have drilled and practiced that particular move in preparation for everything from hostage rescues to escorting prisoners, they wouldn't be so awestruck.*

When he wrapped a large hand around her upper arm and began leading her toward the door, she stiffened, "What are you doing? I'm not ready to leave yet. You can't just manhandle me out of the room you know." Meri's voice was little more than a quiet hiss and Dex wanted to laugh at her lame attempt to avoid being alone with them. *Good luck with that, sweetheart.*

"Be still or we'll chat right here…and I don't think that is in your best interest, do you?" Dex didn't change his expression or slow his pace, he just kept walking. He could see the wrinkles around Ash's eyes—it was usually the only outward sign when the man was enraged—and Dex knew his friend well enough to know he was just a few heartbeats away from giving the gorgeous woman between them a thrashing she'd never forget. If she thought the beating she'd gotten for her comments to Tobi had been bad, she'd be getting one a whole lot worse unless she played her cards very, *very* carefully.

ASH WAS STRAIGHT up pissed off. He wanted to lead Merilee D. Lanham into the nearest housekeeping closet, strip her bare, and beat her ass until she understood there was absolutely no difference between lying with words and deception with silence. But he wasn't going to say one word until he got her through the throng of dignitaries and reporters that seemed to be continually trying to cut off their escape. *The next asshole who tries to step between me and the fucking door is going to get steamrolled.*

There wasn't any doubt that he was mad as hell at Meri, but if Ash was honest—and he always tried to be—he was angrier at himself for not realizing how much more there was to the woman that he and Dex had been spending time with. Talk about your newbie Dom mistake. Hell, this was a beginner-level fuck-up of epic proportions…it might even make it into a training manual or two. When he started to lift his hand to run it through his hair, a gesture even he knew was one of his few *tells*, he cringed at the sharp pain that accompanied the quick movement of his injured arm.

Meri hadn't missed his wince and looked over at him, concern clouding her pretty green eyes. "Are you alright? Oh frog-eating fairies, of course you aren't alright. Damn that was a lame question. What happened to you?" Ash caught the twitch in Dex's jaw and silently willed his friend to keep his mouth shut, he didn't intend to be derailed by explaining his humiliation. God only knew there would be countless retellings of the tale, she could catch one of those.

"This isn't about me. This is about you, pet, and you damn well know it." He almost ran over a couple of rag-tag reporters who thought they would stop if the scrawny pricks stepped into their path...*wrong*. Ash could sense her assistant trailing after them and even with his back to the man, Ash's gay-dar was pinging off the chart. Personally, Ash didn't give a rat's ass what the man's sexual preference was, what occurred between other consenting adults wasn't his concern. What he did care about was the fact the twerp had been so busy flirting with the hospital's CFO that he hadn't been watching out for his boss. "Did you drive here?"

"Yes of course, I dr—"

Ash cut her off with a curt command, "Give me your keys." When she hesitated, he practically growled, "Now, *Meri*." He'd deliberately used the correct pronunciation of her name, and he was sure she hadn't missed the thinly disguised dig. Without even breaking stride, Ash turned and tossed the keys to her assistant. "She'll be with us." Ash could see the muscles in Dex's jaw flexing as he tried not to laugh at the huffing sounds of the man behind them scrambling to retrieve the keys he obviously hadn't managed to catch. *The man has nerd written all over him, not surprised he didn't manage a simple catch, but at least it slows him down a bit. We might actually make it to our truck before he has security on our tails.*

"This isn't at all necessary, you know. We could have easily met somewhere later for coffee and discussed whatever is bothering you." Meri's voice had moved from flustered to indignant. Ash hoped she could hold on to that self-righteous attitude for a while because it would just add to her punishment, and right now he was most certainly in a punishing mood.

"You might want to dial it back a bit, sweetheart, because you're already in a whole peck of trouble." Ash and Dex had been hearing that particular expression their whole lives, but the little wrinkle that appeared between Meri's eyes told him she didn't have a clue what Dex had just said to her...*she'll cipher it out soon 'nuf.* Smiling to himself, he realized the only time he fell back on his southern roots in his speech was when he was dancing on an emotional edge. All his Special Forces training had robbed him of even the slightest hint of his previous southern accent—something his sweet mama had complained endlessly about when he'd first become a SEAL. Now that he was living in Texas, he'd noticed bit by bit his accent was beginning to resurface—yes indeed, his mama was going to be happy as a clam.

Moving quickly through the parking lot toward the pick-up they'd driven, Ash noticed Meri was having trouble keeping up in the heels she was wearing and slowed his pace. Dex must have noticed as well because he'd given Ash's bandaged arm a considering look and all but laughed when Ash slowed. Sure, any other day Ash would have simply scooped Meri up in his arms and continued on, but his damned arm was throbbing like a bitch and he was worried he might actually drop her if he tried his usual Tarzan-routine.

Chapter Four

MERI WAS STARTING to lose patience with their thunderous expressions and curt answers. She'd asked them where they were taking her when they'd pulled out of the hospital's parking lot and Ash's response had been, "If you have anything planned for this evening, cancel it and then hand me your phone." *Presumptuous bastard. And if Tony wrecks my car I'm going to skewer them both. How dare they give him the keys to her baby.* She loved him like a brother, but her assistant was one of the worst driver's ever to sit behind a steering wheel and he'd been nagging her to let him drive her car ever since she'd owned it.

She would have told them she didn't have any plans if they had simply asked, but Ash's barked command grated on her last nerve. Sure she was a submissive, but that didn't mean she was a doormat. *Damn Doms anyway.* Just to be cantankerous, she dialed her private number at the office and left a message explaining she'd been kidnapped by a couple of crazies and the authorities should review the tapes from the presentation at the hospital if her staff hadn't heard from her by morning.

She'd sworn she'd heard them both growl and Dex's hands were now gripping the steering wheel so tight she worried it might snap. The muscles along the side of his jaw clenched so tight she wondered if it might shatter as well. Ash took the phone from her hand, switched it to vibrate, and then slid it into his pocket. "That little stunt will cost you ten." When she turned to glare at him he added, "Be very careful, pet. The tally is already higher than you can cover in one session, you might want to measure your words very carefully." *Sure, threaten me with something I love. What a dumbass. I'm a masochist, you dimwit. I like pain...probably ought to be thinking up something else if you intend to call it punishment.*

Meri had already had her fill of men today so they weren't going to get any huge concessions from her. She'd show them carefully measured words. *Let's see how they like no words at all.* She simply turned and stared out the windshield tuning out everything happening around her. Thinking back over the past few hours, Meri wondered how her life had managed to spiral out of control so quickly. Her assistant, Tony, was the only man she'd been near who hadn't been a total jerk, but even he drained her emotionally. Tony was probably the closest thing Meri had to a best friend, but his love life was such a train wreck the drama surrounding him made the Kardashian's look like they belonged in Mayberry.

The hospital administrator had been propositioning her for months, but he had certainly decided to step up his game today. He'd slid his bear paw sized hand down over her ass when he'd greeted her with a hug that had lasted entirely too long to be considered professional. And when he'd pressed her against a yawn-inspiring erection she'd felt herself shudder, a reaction Meri was certain he'd misinter-preted. If the two jerks sitting on either side of her wanted someone to play the pissy-card with, they could start with him if you asked her. Then, just before the presentation started, two members of the board of directors had sidled up beside her to ask if she'd like to join them at their "clothing optional" retreat this coming weekend. The thought of seeing either of them without clothes made her want to stab herself in the eyes with a blunt instrument. She'd been unable to suppress the small shake that had gone through her as *that* mental picture flashed in her mind again.

And then...the grand finale had been the fiasco with the reporter she'd seen Kelly chatting with. His sneer and expression of barely disguised contempt by the end of the presentation had surprised her. She'd been so lost in trying to figure out why a stranger would dislike her so intensely she'd almost missed his questions. When the words had finally registered, several seconds had passed when all she could do was stare at him with her mouth gaping open in disbelief. She hadn't even been able to form a coherent thought, let alone a response fit for a public venue.

She'd been flustered and Merilee Dillon Lanham *did not do* flustered...well at least she never had before she'd learned two of her childhood acquaintances had opened a kink club just outside of Austin. Meri's entire life had been centered on being groomed to follow in her father's footsteps. Business journals all over the country were referring to her as "Fundraising's Golden Girl". She was well on her way to establishing herself as one of the nation's top foundation leaders. And through all those years of preparation for this role, her mother hadn't let Meri's business education push aside or overshadow all her earlier lessons in gentility either. Diana Dillon-Lanham made sure her daughter knew exactly how to present a public persona that was precisely what everyone expected...and Meri had performed flawlessly until the day she'd gotten up the courage and called Kent West.

Even though their parents ran in the same social circles, Meri had never known either Kyle or Kent well, but their paths had crossed often enough over the years that Meri knew Kent was the more approachable of the two. It had only taken her a few days to discretely set up their lunch meeting. Thinking back on that day still sent a flash of embarrassment through her and she hoped the two men sitting beside her were too caught up in their anger to notice. "Want to share that thought, pet? And I'll advise you to give your fondness for *editing* some serious reconsideration." Ash's words might have sounded casual, but the steel under them was pure command. *Damn Dom thinks he can just waltz in and make demands like he's the king of all he surveys. As if...*

She took a minute to think through the wisdom of the snark that had initially popped into her head and decided this wasn't a battlefield worth dying on. Meri took a deep breath and sighed. "I was just remembering how hard it had been to call Kent West when I first heard about the club he and Kyle had opened. I met him for lunch and it was...well, let's just say it was an interesting conversation." She'd wanted to meet at Uchi, but Kent had just laughed and told her that raw fish was bait. Meri hadn't been surprised when he'd suggested Jeffrey's, it was an upscale establishment, and served enough steak and potato fare to keep even the purest Texas heart happy. Add in the gorgeous bar and it was perfect. In the end she'd been grateful because a happy, relaxed dinner companion was much easier to talk to than one who was continually frowning at his plate.

"Why did you call Kent? Were you friends?" She knew Ash had tried to keep his questions nonchalant, but she hadn't missed the tinge of jealousy he'd tried to suppress.

"Not really, but we were acquaintances. Our families'

circles of friends overlap some, so we've all known one another for years. You don't have to know Kent and Kyle well to be able to see Kent is the more personable. And since I was already nervous about the meeting…well, you know." She felt her face heat again and cursed the fact she blushed so easily even though she always looked like she'd just returned from the tropics. She had her dad to thank for her perpetual tan and dark hair, but her sparkling green eyes had definitely been a gift from her mom.

Meri felt her heart clench when she thought about her parents. God she missed them even though they'd only been gone a few weeks, but on days like today it seemed like forever. Taking a deep breath to push back the tears she felt starting to fill her eyes, Meri tried to focus on how much the two people she loved the most deserved this time of freedom. This past year they had actually been gone on so many "adventures" as her mom called them, that Meri was finally—reluctantly, very reluctantly— starting to adjust to being alone in the enormous home they all shared. Granted she had lived in the mansion's west wing since she'd been sixteen. Her mom had called it "Autonomy Training". Meri smiled as she thought back on all the different parenting strategies her mom had tried. Through it all, her dad had just smiled and continued to listen and guide with a steadfast consistency that had given Meri the foundation to become the woman she was now. Her mom had given her imagination and wings, she'd opened her daughter's mind to trying new things, but her dad was the one who had always been rock solid.

Glancing to the side, Meri saw Ash watching her, studying her as if he'd be able to figure out what she was thinking if he just looked closely enough. And for just a sliver of a moment she wondered if it might be right. She'd never been good at deceit, and even though she had known Dex and Ash weren't aware of who she was, it hadn't been a problem because their confusion hadn't been due to any deception on her part. They had made a number of wrong assumptions without bothering to find out more about her. And if she had to guess, she'd put her money on the fact they were actually more angry at themselves, but it was just easier to take their frustrations out on her. She had no intention of letting them off that easy. They were making a big mistake letting her have so much time to stew over this...yes indeed, a very big mistake. The longer she thought about it the more downhill her attitude was sliding. *You want my respect outside of the club, asshats? Earn it.*

DEX MIGHT HAVE been driving but that didn't mean he was oblivious to the anger beginning to radiate off the woman sitting close enough he could feel the warmth of her sweet body. He knew Ash's arm had to be throbbing like a bitch, but dammit, the man had been a SEAL, so a little bit of pain was no reason to act like a jerk. And despite his attempts to disguise it, Dex had seen Ash's eyes practically turn green with jealousy when Meri had mentioned calling Kent about the club. Personally he was thanking God above she'd made that call, otherwise they might have never met her, and despite their rough start, Dex really did enjoy her company. They hadn't spent a lot of time together in social situations, but those few times had given him a glimpse of the woman aside from the sub they loved playing with at Prairie Winds. And what he'd seen today had upped the stakes of his interest exponentially.

Time for some damage control. "Tell us about the new hospital wing, Meri. We aren't far from our destination, but it sounds like a really ambitious undertaking and I'm interested in hearing about it." Dex was headed to a small overlook a few miles from the club. He'd decided a neutral setting was best and since this spot was on private property, they would all be able to speak openly without worrying about being overheard. He was glad to see some of the tension drain away as she started telling them about the vision she and her parents shared for community improvement. She said her dad's entire career had been spent managing the family's charitable foundation. She'd followed in his footsteps, getting her MBA from Harvard and then starting in an entry-level position.

By the time they'd parked the truck under one of the sprawling oak trees, Meri and Ash seemed to have calmed down and Dex was surprised at the relief he felt about that. There had been a small part of him that had worried Ash was going to blow their chances with her, and this was the first time it had ever mattered. It wasn't that Dex wasn't frustrated, but since he'd had a chance to step back a bit, he'd been able to see he was actually far more frustrated with himself than he was with her. That didn't mean she hadn't earned a punishment round or two, but they'd have to be careful because the woman was a borderline masochist and most traditional punishments were actually rewards for her.

"Where are we?" The sun just getting ready to settle behind the horizon and the first stars were beginning to sparkle in the violet sky. It would be dark soon and he understood her trepidation. She'd basically been kidnapped by two men she knew were angry with her and taken to a hillside overlooking the river, and they'd taken her phone away from her. Dex would have been more upset if she hadn't asked, because even though they'd never hurt her beyond the limits they all still respected, it wasn't something she should assume outside of a club setting.

The club had a zero tolerance policy for anyone not following the BDSM lifestyle tenet *Safe, Sane, and Consensual,* but Meri couldn't be sure those same rules still applied here. At Prairie Winds, any applicant who wasn't completely on board with that policy was denied membership; it was just that simple. But the truth of it was the vetting process for prospective members was so stringent and thorough, it was rarely an issue. During the months he and Ash had been working there, they'd only seen dungeon monitors step into a scene a few times, and each of those had been at the Dom's request. It wasn't unusual when a Dom was new or topping a sub they didn't know well, to ask a more experienced Top for suggestions—or at least it wasn't unusual for the *smart ones* to ask for guidance.

Dex turned in his seat so Meri would be able to see him clearly. It was important she understood that no matter what the outcome of their discussion, she would always be safe in their care. "We are on a small acreage of private property not far from the club. It's quiet here and we won't have to worry about being overheard." He saw a small flash of something too close to fear flash in her eyes and he realized she'd misunderstood what he'd been trying to say. "What I was trying to say, sweetness, was that we would all be able to speak freely without being concerned about being overheard. If we'd met in a coffee shop as you'd suggested earlier, we wouldn't have been about to speak as openly as we can here." He paused to study her expression, wanting to avoid any further miscommunication. "You know you are safe with us, right?"

Ash's face turned sharply toward him and his eyebrows furrowed as he considered Meri might actually be worried about her safety. If there was one thing Dex knew about his friend, it was that despite the fact Ash considered himself a sadist, he would never intentionally harm a woman in a way they hadn't all agreed to before starting a scene. Ash was meticulous about the well-being of all submissives and had always been practically obsessive when it came to Meri. Hell, Dex had often accused Ash of negotiating scenes to death because he'd scripted scenes so tight there hadn't been any spontaneity left at all, and the result had often been scenes that were as flat as yesterday's open beer.

Dex could see Ash was barely breathing as he waited for Meri to answer. When she finally nodded her head, they both let out the breaths they'd been holding. "I'm glad you asked where we are, sweetheart. Your safety is always going to be our first concern and it should be yours as well. We'll never punish you for asking questions related to your safety—but we'll reserve the right to punish you anytime you *don't* take care of yourself." Even in the fading sunlight, Dex could see her muscles relax ever so slightly at the familiar words. Any Dom worth his salt insisted any submissive in his or her care was to take their safety seriously. Dex opened the door and reached for Meri's hand, "Come. We need to talk, but we want to show you something first."

Standing at the edge of the rock wall edging the river, Dex heard Meri's sharp intake of breath as she looked out over the vista below. They weren't particularly high, but the wide-open view was spectacular. From where he'd parked, she wouldn't have been able to see any of the spectacular features of the property, so they'd moved quickly into a position to see the setting sun paint the sky with shades of pink and orange that were quickly fading into deeper shades as they shifted to violet. Mother Nature was showing off this evening and it was breathtaking.

Dex saw Meri's eyes widen when she looked around, he had expected her to appreciate the view, but he hadn't expected her to look up at him with tears in her eyes. "It's amazing. I never take time to enjoy things like this anymore and I should." She must have seen his confusion because she pointed to the mansion on the next hilltop, "That's where I live. Well, specifically I live in the west wing, my parents live in the east wing. This view is available to me every night from the balcony off my bedroom, but I don't take the time to enjoy it."

Dex watched as Ash stepped up behind Meri and wrapped his arms around her, "And you think by not enjoying it, you're being wasteful." It hadn't been a question, but Dex had seen her nod anyway. Typically, Dex was the one who comforted the subs in their care while Ash pushed them, but there was something special about Merilee Lanham, and it warmed his heart to see a softer side of Ash emerging.

While Ash held Meri, Dex looked at the enormous home belonging to Meri's family. What they hadn't yet told her was the two of them had purchased this land a few months earlier. They were in the process of designing a "green" home and hoped to break ground on the project sometime in the next year. They'd wondered about the owners of the sprawling mansion because they would eventually become their nearest neighbors, and now that he knew—he wasn't sure if he was relieved or worried.

Dex was glad neither Meri nor Ash seemed as keyed up as they had been earlier. He watched her slip off the four-inch heels she'd been wearing and lean back stretching out the muscles of her neck and back. They all sat dangling their legs over the edge of the sheer rock face that dropped to the river below. For just a few moments Dex felt as if they were all teens enjoying a night at Lookout Point back home. Sadly, his and Ash's years as Navy SEALs had changed them. They were no longer the idealistic young men who had started Basic together, so sure they could change the world. They'd both become jaded in a lot of ways over the years. Dex hadn't realized how much he'd changed until he'd returned home one Christmas. He'd been leaning against the back wall of his parents' large living room watching the chaos when his sister, Lizzy, stepped up to him and smiled warmly. He'd instinctively shaken the hand she'd extended but he'd been completely confused when she'd introduced herself.

When he'd asked, "What's this about, Lizzy? You know exactly who I am."

"No, I don't think I do. You look like my little brother, but when I look into *your* eyes, I don't see *him*." He'd been too stunned to respond. She'd looked at him cautiously, but had finally added, "If you see him, would you please tell him that I love him…we all do. And that we miss him very much and that we hope he'll find his way back to us soon."

Dex still remembered feeling as if he'd been sucker punched. It had been a life-changing moment and he'd wondered for just a few seconds if he'd been hit by lightning standing right in the middle of his parents' home. Elizabeth was seven years older than Dex and she'd always considered herself his second mother, so he wasn't surprised she was taking him to task. What tore at his heart was the absolute truth of her words. From then on, Dex had made a sincere effort to conceal the way his career was changing him—at least he'd tried to hide the worst of it from his family.

Oddly enough, the more he'd consciously set aside the turbulence he felt in his soul, the calmer he'd actually become. He and several other teammates had been discussing the efforts they had to make to hide the atrocities of war from their loved ones one night after returning from a particularly difficult mission. The whiskey had loosened them up enough they'd actually broached an emotional topic for a change. One of the men's wives had quietly said, "Created reality." When he'd questioned her, she had gone on to explain how we choose our reality by allowing or disallowing certain thoughts to occupy our minds.

Dex had stared at her as the absolute truth of her words hit him like a Mack truck. She'd just smiled shyly and said, "You hold all the power you know...you can let all the horrible things you see taint your future or you can learn from them...it's always your choice." He'd been stunned by the simplicity of her words and the fact two different women had sensed how emotionally adrift he'd been was more than a little humbling.

Looking at Meri—her eyes so filled with wonder and appreciation of the beauty surrounding her, Dex couldn't help feel she held his heart in her hand already, but neither of them had been notified yet. *Oh brother, you really have fucking lost it and if Ash gets wind you've detoured into the deep end of the romance pool, there will be no living with him.* Dex finally broke the silence by saying, "Tell us why you didn't tell us who you are." He knew his comment lacked any sort of finesse, but the words had tumbled out before he'd had the chance to polish them.

Chapter Five

M ERI HEARD SEVERAL different underlying emotions in Dex's demand for an explanation, but the one that surprised her the most was hurt. It had never occurred to her that he and Ash might be offended by her duplicity. It wasn't as if she had intentionally kept the information from them, and in truth, they likely knew they shared more than a little bit of the responsibility. They hadn't been interested enough to ask questions, so why was *he* offended? *Well, I didn't grow up in Texas without learning a thing or two about game-day strategy and every Cowboy's fan knows that sometimes the best defense is a good offense.* She took a deep breath and looked out over the darkening sky, "Well, if you will think back, I'm sure you'll realize you rarely expressed much interest in idle chit-chat. And I'm not sure exactly when I would have worked the details of my financial portfolio into the time we've spent together."

She hadn't intended to sound quite so snippy, and the sudden tension in the air told her it was time to tone it down a little. "I used my first and middle names on my club membership to fly under the radar as much as possible. I'm sure you can see why that was important. And I've used it before for travel because I don't always take personal protection with me and security is sometimes an issue." *And wasn't that an enormous understatement at the moment.* She had purposely tried to keep her reference to security challenges vague, but in her peripheral vision Meri had seen both men swivel their faces to her.

"Excuse me?" *Oh brother.* Ash's voice had sounded almost menacing and suddenly Meri was grateful for the encroaching darkness. "You wanna run that by us again, pet? Because that sounded a lot like you've had some security issues and I don't remember hearing them mentioned either. You really do seem to be racking up punishments at an astonishing rate."

Dex leaned closer and asked, "Have you mentioned this to anyone? Anyone at all? Because I have to tell you, I have a bad feeling about this. That little pissant reporter was fed information by someone and you need to take *any* security issues you're having very seriously. Just because your foundation does good work doesn't mean you won't make enemies along the way." *And isn't that a fact? Damn, this conversation is sliding downhill fast.*

"Listen, I'm not discounting my safety, but I'm not going to get bogged-down with paranoia either. If I let every threatening email and security breach at the mansion get to me, I'd have become a recluse years ago." Instead of easing their tension, her words seemed to have ratcheted it up even further. "I had planned to talk to Micah and Jax, but I haven't had a chance to speak with them yet." When she heard Ash growl, Meri shook her head and sighed. Obviously he was remembering they had all been together just a few days ago. Sighing, she added, "Yes, I know we were all at the gazebo recently, but I didn't want to bring it up in front of everyone."

This time Dex was the one who seemed incredulous, "By everyone, I'm assuming you mean the two of us?" *Oh brother, talk about a no-win question. If I answer honestly, they'll misunderstand. And if I lie, they'll know.*

Meri took another deep breath and looked up at the stars as if they might suddenly decide to shower her with a brilliant answer. "It wasn't that I didn't want you to know—precisely. It was more that I didn't want you to feel obligated to help. And whether or not you are willing to admit it, it is exactly what would have happened." *Hell's bells and seashells, that's exactly what's happening now. And if they will just step back for a minute they'll know it, too.* She might not have been looking directly at them in the bright light of day, but the energy vibrating around them was screaming overprotection. Meri wondered if all Doms were like this or just the ones in her circle of friends. Maybe it was those who were former military or former Special Forces who were also Doms, although she suspected that was a chicken and egg argument as well since every member of any branch of the Special Forces Meri had ever met, seemed to be a Dom. Sighing, she finally decided it was a question for Dan.

Only a few people knew how close she and Dr. Dan Deal really were. And even fewer knew their family connection. Dan's mother and Meri's mom were sisters, and when her aunt and uncle were killed by a drunk driver just after Dan started high school, the Lanhams immediately moved the young man into their home. Meri hadn't even started junior high school yet, but she and her older cousin bonded quickly. He'd been her protector and best pal until he'd moved to college four years later.

Meri wished her sweet cousin would find a woman who deserved his affection. He was one of the nicest men she knew and even though he was a sexual Dominant, he didn't seem the type of Dom who would want to control every aspect of his sub's life. It wasn't that he couldn't be overly protective at times, because he certainly had taken her to task for some of the poor choices she'd made while in college. He'd always reserved his lectures for the mistakes he'd seen as *dumb* rather than dangerous. Dan had always encouraged her to push beyond what she thought she could do academically and professionally. She had often wished she had a dollar for every time he'd reminded her "the worst you can do is fail."

She'd been in high school when she'd decided to run for a student government position at her posh private school. She had lost the election by a narrow margin and been devastated. Dan had been home that weekend and found her crying in her dad's office. He'd listened quietly as she'd poured out her heart, asking her questions that she'd figured out later had gently led her to figure out all on her own what he'd known all along...that in the great scheme of things, this was a small bump in the road. He'd eventually donned her dad's old felt Fedora and started singing the old Frank Sinatra classic, "Pick Yourself Up". The words still echoed in her head whenever she felt like she'd failed. *So take a deep breath – Pick yourself up – Dust yourself off – Start all over again.*

"I'm not sure whether to be pissed off or encouraged by the fact she isn't answering the question." Dex's voice broke through the tune playing in Meri's head and she frantically searched her memory hoping to remember what he'd asked her. "I know that expression, sweetheart. I'm fairly certain you didn't even hear me ask you when you had planned to talk to Jax or Micah, so you might as well stop wasting all that energy searching your memory."

Meri let out a breath she hadn't even realized she was holding and felt herself sag. In the back of her mind, Meri wondered why she was fighting this battle when it was so obviously in vain. "I have a business trip coming up in a few days. My hope is whoever is doing this will lose interest and move on while I'm gone. I promise to call them if I'm still having trouble when I return." Despite what everyone might think, her life really was incredibly boring. Even her weekly trips to the Prairie Winds Club had begun to dwindle under the mounting pressures of her career. And she'd also started worrying about trouble following her there as well. Quite frankly, the fear that someone else might be caught up in her mess was the stuff of nightmares.

"Well, pet, I think perhaps you need to start at the beginning. And don't leave anything out." Ash's voice was pitched lower than she'd ever heard it and sounded even more menacing than his usual Dom-voice, and just the sound of it sent a shiver of apprehension up her spine. And if the two of them thought they were *miffed* before, they were going to be positively livid when she told them about the trouble she'd been having recently.

ASH'S JAW WAS ready to crack under the strain—clenching his mouth closed might be keeping him from spewing curses like the sailor he'd been, but it was going to cost him a fucking fortune in dental work. The more Merilee Lanham talked, the more difficult it was to keep from asking the most basic question…*Why haven't you asked for help?* Of course that question would lead to a hundred others, including…*What made you think this would just go away?*

He and Dex listened as Meri recounted how she'd started getting text messages to her private cell phone the day after her parents left for South America. The messages hadn't been particularly threatening in the beginning, but they had been fairly frequent. When she didn't respond, the sender had begun including photos of her that had been taken during unguarded moments. A few had shown her walking from the parking garage to her downtown office, others had been taken during her quick lunch breaks. She'd known they were current pictures because she'd recognized the clothing she'd worn on the days she'd eaten in specific locations. Once she started watching for someone taking her picture, they'd abruptly stopped.

"I really thought it was over, because I hadn't gotten anything for a couple of days...but then I started getting emails to my personal account." Ash was watching her closely or he might have missed the small shiver that moved through her before she continued, "This time the pictures were taken from a distance, enough so some were a bit grainy. You know, like they'd been taken using a high-powered zoom lens. One showed me driving through the gates at Prairie Winds and another was taken later that night when I'd been standing out on the terrace behind the club. There were more over the course of several days' activities, but you get the idea."

"Is this why you haven't been to the club much in the past few weeks?"

For the first time since they'd started talking, Ash saw a very real sadness move through her expression. Thinking back, he could only recall one other time he'd sensed anything other than a positive vibe from Meri and that told him a lot about who she was at her core. "Truthfully, that is a part of it but not all. My responsibilities at the Foundation are growing faster than my ability to acclimate and delegate...and with my dad gone, well, things are even more insane than usual."

One of the things Ash had noticed was the fact she appeared to have lost weight—not a lot, but enough to let him know she was probably stumbling into her home late at night when she was far too exhausted to do any more than fall into bed. If she belonged to them, he and Dex would make damned sure she took better care of herself. *For a sadist you seem to be getting pretty fucking sappy.* Shocked at the direction of his thoughts, Ash decided talking to himself probably wasn't really a bad sign until he started carrying on both sides of the conversation.

Ash had the feeling she hadn't told them everything yet and when he looked over her head at Dex, he saw the almost imperceptible shake of his head. Obviously Dex had the same idea, so they would just wait her out. It was several long minutes before she finally continued, "There was a break-in at my home a few days ago. I'd sent the staff all home because I was just *done*, you know?" They waited while she took a couple of deep breaths and sighed. A part of him wanted to shake her until her teeth rattled, but there was also a small part of him that understood exactly what she was saying. He'd felt much the same way after missions that hadn't gone well. "Have you ever been so tired and lonely that all you wanted was to be alone and drown it all in alcohol?" When they'd both snorted and nodded in understanding, she went on, "Well, that was where I was that day. Anyway, the perimeter alarms are the oldest of the security on the estate, so they went off just a few seconds before the house alarms started wailing. I didn't hear my phone ring when the security company called because I was soaking in a bubble bath, and while I was busy scrambling for a robe, I slipped and fell."

Dex heard her soft laugh and saw her shaking her head, but the moonlight was bright enough he saw her eyes had filled with tears and knew how frantic she must have felt. "Hell, on my best day I can be a klutz, but that night was even over the top for me. I'm still wearing long sleeves to hide all the bruises, and we won't even talk about the other places that are black and blue. Anyway, by the time the police arrived, there wasn't anyone to be found and nothing was missing that I've been able to find. The only thing *wrong* was there was a small bouquet of monkshood laying in the center of the dining room table."

"What the fuck?" Dex's confusion echoed Ash's own bewilderment.

"See? I didn't know either, but one of the female officers Googled it and evidently it means 'You'd better watch your back'. Who knows that kind of thing? I mean really, what kind of sick piece of navel lint sits around figuring out something like that?"

Meri finally reluctantly conceded the situation had gotten out of control and she needed help, and despite the fact he'd found her reference to her stalker as a piece of lint amusing, Ash found himself barely being able to hold back his anger. And finding out Parker Andrews had been one of the officers called to her home the night of the break-in hadn't done anything for Ash's good humor either. He planned to have a nice long chat with his fellow Dom about the importance of sharing information. *Well, fuck!* At least he had planned to have a come-to-Jesus meeting with Master Andrews until he realized neither he nor Dex had any real claim on Meri. Even though they had been playing with her exclusively since they'd met, they hadn't made any public declarations—hell, they hadn't even made a private commitment to her. For just a moment Ash wondered how that had impacted her decision to try to handle this situation on her own.

Ash wasn't the "people person" Dex was, but he felt certain her submissive training would have kicked in if she'd felt more secure in their relationship. At the very least she would have called them after the break-in because she had to know Parker Andrews would eventually share the information. It didn't seem to matter how he looked at it, the bottom line was, Ms. Lanham wasn't solely responsible for this mess. And somehow, punishing her for a situation they'd helped create just didn't seem right.

Dex's question broke through his musing, "Any idea who might want to hurt you, sweetheart?"

"Well, if you are asking me if I have any enemies, I can only think of a couple of people who really dislike me. But would it be enough to want to really hurt me? I just can't see either of them going that far. I mean, they would both lose everything if they were caught and I honestly think their egos would stand in the way of that. Not to mention they'd see it as beneath them to have to do anything *dirty* themselves, and hiring someone else sets them up to be blackmailed later."

The last fragments of daylight had finally faded from the sky, but Meri's face was illuminated by the full moon, highlighting her perfect features and giving her skin a soft glow that made her look almost ethereal. Even in the dim light, Ash could easily see her wrinkled brow and knew she was trying to decide how much more information to share.

"Let me help you out with your decision, pet. Spill it all—don't hold anything back, even if you think it is something we really don't want to hear. We can't help if we don't have all the Intel." Ash hoped she'd make the connection between their ability to help and their former jobs as Navy SEALs. Having all the available information usually meant the difference between success and failure.

And when failure means people die—you have to develop a very high regard for those who supply your Intelligence. He saw her draw in a deep breath and could almost feel the last bit of fight drain away as she resigned herself to telling them everything. Just as she opened her mouth to speak, her phone starting vibrating and then ringing in his pocket.

"That's my dad's ringtone. It overrides the vibrate only setting. He wasn't supposed to call until Sunday night, so I need to answer that." Ash reluctantly handed over the jiggling device and listened as she greeted her father. "Hey, Dad, what's up? Is everything all right?"

Ash could hear her father's rapid-fire words, but was only able to make out a few. The longer Meri listened the more visibly upset she became, she was quickly on her feet and moving toward the pickup. She'd forgotten her shoes and Ash knew from experience the rocks they'd spread on the road had to be shredding the bottoms of her delicate feet. He grabbed her shoes and struggled to get to his feet, biting back the urge to curse out loud at the pain that shot up his forearm when he pressed against the dirt to stand up. Dex was already on the move and scooped her up without ever missing a step, his long stride eating up the last few yards between them and his truck in a couple of seconds.

As the motor caught, Ash heard Meri repeat the fact she was safe and her promise to call her dad with an update on Tony as soon as she found out his condition. *Tony? The man I tossed her keys to when we left the hospital? What could have happened to him in such a short period of time that would have her dad calling from South America?*

Chapter Six

AFTER DEX SET Merilee on the seat, he'd gently pried the phone from her shaking fingers and slid it into his shirt pocket before scooting her into the center seat and fastening her safety belt. He smoothed her hair back from her face and double-checked that he'd heard their destination correction. She was white as a sheet and he wanted nothing more than to hold her against him and assure her everything was going to be all right. But since he had no way of knowing that was true, and he wouldn't mislead her, he kept quiet. He planned to return a call to Merilee's dad as soon as they reached the hospital he'd heard her mention. Damn if it wasn't the same facility they'd just left a couple of hours ago. They hadn't gone far when traffic slowed to a crawl. He was nearly blinded by all the flashing lights, but he'd glanced over to see a small red sports car that looked like it had been put through a metal compactor. Hearing Meri's gasp was all the confirmation Dex needed that the mangled ball of metal was what little was left of her car.

When he glanced over at Ash, his friend gave a quick jerk of his head to their right and Dex caught sight of the unmistakable lights of a chopper moving off into the distance. They had evidently airlifted the driver away from the scene and that didn't bode well for the man's condition. They moved past the snarled traffic at a snail's pace and

Dex was relieved to hear Ash talking softly to Meri, reassuring her they would get her to her friend's side as quickly as they safely could. Dex had no intention of making an already difficult situation even more so by taking unnecessary risks.

By the time they reached the small trauma center their phones had been ringing almost continually as word spread that Meri's car had been involved in a bad accident. Austin might be a large city, but the Prairie Winds community was much smaller and well connected enough that word had spread through the members like wild fire. Dex had been impressed the call that seemed to have settled Meri the most had been from Tobi West. *Sure wouldn't have predicted that.* Dex's respect for his bosses' wife seemed to grow each time he had an encounter with her. The way she had forgiven Meri unconditionally and defended her when other club members hadn't been so charitable had spoken volumes about her character.

Walking in to the small hospital's emergency department made Dex think about all the old Carol Burnett Shows he'd watched on late night television as a kid. The entire area was filled with people in various stages of frustration. Dean and Dell West were standing at the nurse's station and, judging by the look on the older nurse's face, that conversation wasn't going particularly well. A couple of reporters spotted Meri right away and made a mad dash in her direction. He and Ash moved to block the circling sharks and their snarling finally discouraged the news hounds. The reporters finally slunk back against the wall, but Dex knew they'd only won a small skirmish, the real war hadn't even started yet. Turning back to Meri, he pulled her against his chest and just held her. He was stunned to feel her shaking to the point he wasn't sure how much longer she'd be able to stand before her knees gave out.

He and Ash had worked together so long their communication often required little more than a quick nod, so when Dex saw his friend's eyes dart to the waiting room he began to lead Meri in that direction. Ash strode off toward the nurses' station and Dex hoped his friend would summon some of the charm and tact he probably wasn't feeling because pissing off the nurse Dean and Dell were already haggling with wasn't going to be all that difficult. And getting kicked out wasn't going to help Meri at all. Dex had almost gotten Meri through the sliding doors of the waiting room when they heard a loud shriek followed by a man's excited voice saying, "Honey, if you plan to put your hands on me *there,* you need a mani. What do you do—sand wood with your bare hands?"

Dex was grateful he already had an arm wrapped around Meri because he'd barely registered her softly whispered words, "Oh thank God" before her knees folded out from under her. Scooping her up in his arms, he quickly made his way to a chair and cradled her in his lap. It wasn't difficult to determine the voice she'd heard was her assistant and if he was chastising someone for the condition of their hands, he probably wasn't mortally injured.

"Are you alright? I hope that was your assistant we heard, because I'm pretty sure he isn't going to die from being chafed by someone's rough hands."

"Yes, I'm fine, but thank you for not letting me make a scene by dropping like a stone. And yes, that was Tony, and I agree with you that he must be doing okay if he is saying things that are so typical of him." He could almost feel her relief but her relaxed state was destined to be short-lived.

"Ms. Lanham, who was driving your car? Would you like to comment on the rumor your car was sabotaged? And is this your new boyfriend? Is he the reason you and the Senator broke up?" Dex hadn't even seen the man step up in front of them until he started firing questions at Meri. And the minute the woman next to him jumped on-board the whole room became instant chaos. There were several camera flashes and more shouted questions when Dex saw the Wests and Ash stalk into the room. What had been chaos quickly degenerated in to full-blown FUBAR. And if he was honest, Dex would have to say fucked up beyond all recognition was an understatement.

THE PHOTOGRAPHER STOOD by shrieking about her rights while Ash calmly deleted all the photos of the accident scene, which included a close-up shot of Meri's tag—he didn't even want to think about what she'd planned to do with that picture. The pictures of Meri and Dex were also gone with a few quick presses of a button, he then double-checked the device's backup. *Oh yeah, saw this one coming. Good try, Lois Lane, but Navy SEALs are smarter than the average bear.* The woman shouted something about him destroying her personal property and he laughed. "Listen, if you intend to blame me for destroying your camera then you can bet your sweet ass I'm going to get the privilege. So as I see it you have two choices, shut up or watch me *fix* your camera so there won't even be salvageable parts left." He leaned closer to her and snarled, "I deleted twenty-two pictures out of the fifteen hundred and sixty-two you had. How would you like to lose them all, honey?" He had deliberately leaned over her, making sure he towered over her in the process.

Parker Andrews sauntered in the door, took in the brewing trouble, and casually inquired, "Anyone know who has a dark green Honda Civic? I think I saw one being towed out of the lot." The reporter and photographer both gasped and clamored from the room with the others in their wake. "Of course I could be wrong," he added quietly after the doors slid shut behind them. His smile was pure wicked delight and Ash couldn't help but laugh at how quickly, and effectively the detective had managed to solve the problem. He turned and looked down at Meri, "Don't worry, Merilee, we've got people at all the entrances now, they won't be getting back in until we're ready to let them."

Everybody in the room seemed to settle back and Ash watched as Meri sagged in relief. "Thanks. I really didn't want anyone else pulled into this, but I'm not sure how I can avoid it now."

Jax McDonald stepped forward, crossed his arms over his chest, and looked down at Meri with narrowed eyes. "I just got off the phone with your dad, Merilee. To say he was worried would be an understatement as you can well imagine." Ash watched as Meri visibly cringed. Since the Wests, McDonalds, and Lanhams were all wealthy locals, it stood to reason they would all be connected socially. *Fuck it. Did everybody in the damned club know who she was but us?*

"Want to explain to me why I'm hearing about this from your dad and not you, sweetness? And give your answer some serious thought because I'm damned mad right now." Glancing around before refocusing his attention on Meri, the new father added, "Deaga has decided three hours of sleep every night is plenty, I swear the kid was a damned BUD/S trainer in a previous life, so I'm tired and cranky, and looking for a target so you best not put your ass on the line—and I mean that literally."

Ash felt every muscle in his body stiffen as the familiar feeling of adrenaline rushing through him readied his body for a fight. *What the hell? He threatens her ass right in front of us?* And his earlier realization that they didn't really have any real claim on her twisted uneasily in his gut, and from the scowl on Dex's face, Ash figured his partner was facing the same unpleasant awareness. Ash hadn't ever been one of those Doms that subs cuddled up against. He'd always had a very specific role when he and Dex shared scenes and he'd been completely content with the status quo, until they'd met Meri. Christ, if he wasn't careful he was going to go soft like Kyle and Micah. He nearly groaned at the thought of becoming less than the Dom he knew Meri needed. He and Dex were the perfect combination for her, and he hoped they hadn't missed their window of opportunity to convince her of that.

Chapter Seven

M ERILEE SAT BETWEEN Dex and Ash wondering how the Masters of the Prairie Winds Club had managed to manipulate her into agreeing to let the two Doms flanking her move into her home. The only reasonable excuse she could come up with was she'd been so relieved and grateful when she'd seen for herself Tony was going to be fine, she probably would have agreed to let the devil himself move in. *Who are you kidding? For all intents and purposes, that is exactly what you have done—times two.* Groaning to herself, Meri had to hold back her urge to smack her palm against her forehead. *This is going to be a disaster of biblical proportions.* Taking a quick mental inventory of her wing of the house, she worked out which bedrooms she could put both of them in. They would be close, but not too close.

Tony was going to be spending a day or two at the hospital since they'd needed to pin the breaks in his leg. Meri smiled thinking about her assistant. When he'd been moved back into his room, it had been obvious the lingering effects of the anesthetic had made him a flirty sexpot who had drawn male staff like a magnet. The hospital's CFO had nearly gone postal and chased away the other would-be suitors, claiming they were a security risk. Tony had batted his long lashes at the man asking, "How can they be a security risk when they already work here?"

When the CFO had blushed, Tony had added, "I think you just want me all to yourself, don't you?" Meri had snorted a laugh before covering it with a cough and turning her face into Dex's shoulder. Even though Tony was going to make a full recovery, he was going to need some special attention for a couple of weeks and Meri had been pleased to know the CFO had taken a keen interest in helping. Even though she didn't know Shane Oak personally, all of the business dealings she'd had with him indicated he was competent, honest, and pleasant. It wasn't a perfect personal recommendation, but it was a good start.

When Jax had confronted her about the trouble she'd been having, every Dom in the damned waiting room had gone on point. She'd have sworn they were all a bunch of bird dogs the way they'd frozen and turned their noses toward her. *Yep, probably better keep that bird dog analogy to myself, pretty sure I'm already in enough trouble... again!* Why did it seem the harder she tried the worse her decisions seemed to be when all was said and done? At the time it always seemed like she had perfectly good reasoning for a choice, but then someone else would question her logic and they never seemed to understand how her mind had worked something through. More than once her dad had asked her to walk him through her thought process when she'd been a teenager. And more often than not he'd just sat behind his desk and stared at her looking completely befuddled, much like Jax had done this evening.

He hadn't agreed with her assessment of the situation not being a problem until recently and he'd been even less impressed with her observation that hindsight was twenty-twenty. And now that she thought back on it, Meri was relatively certain she'd heard Dex and Ash both growl something about penalties for bratty behavior and insolence, but she'd ignored them. She hadn't been trying to be disrespectful—well, not particularly—"dissing" them, as the younger aids at the foundation referred to it, was more of a bonus really. She had meant what she said…it's easy to judge someone else's decision when you have all the information and the luxury of time and perspective. Jax's reaction had been blown completely out of proportion and she'd told him so. That had set off a virtual "shit-storm" the likes of which Meri hadn't seen in a long time. Evidently telling a Dom he needed a nap was not considered appropriate because she could swear she'd seen steam come out his ears.

None of them had stopped to think that she was bone tired, and by the time Jax had jumped down her throat she'd been on the backside of an adrenaline crash. He was probably lucky she hadn't launched into a rant that would have shocked them all to their toes. At least this way they were simply pissed. Sighing to herself, she refocused on figuring out the accommodations for the two "guests" she would have until Jax could get the security system upgraded. Of course the chances of him hurrying the upgrades along were probably pretty slim now…*damn it.*

Just as Dex parked in front of the house the front door opened and both Carl Phillips and Peter Weston stepped out. Even though she hadn't known they were there, Meri wasn't particularly surprised to see them. Her housekeeper, Hattie, was ordinarily positively anal about denying strangers access to the house, but Hattie knew Jax and would have happily opened the door to the devil himself if he'd asked her to. *Traitor.* Watching the two recently retired SEALs move down the wide front stairs like the predators they were made her think comparing them to devils might not be that far off the mark.

Meri nodded to the two men but didn't stop to listen to what she was certain was going to be their report on the sorry state of her security "protocols" as Jax had called them. *Protocols? Really?* And telling her that stacking up her mama's crystal stemware in front of the door would have done more good than her current alarm system was just being an ass. She heard Peter Weston snort with laughter as she stepped through the door. *Fuck me clear to next Friday, I forgot he's a damned empath.*

Regi had warned her about him, but Tobi had been the one who had made the biggest impression. She'd sworn Peter was responsible for the worst paddling she'd ever gotten. Evidently her sweet smile had hidden her inner tantrum from Kent and Kyle, but Peter had joined them in one of the casual sitting areas at the club and had thrown her under the bus. "He started asking me questions and in about thirty seconds it was painfully, and I mean that literally, he'd obviously heard all the plans my mind had been working on." When Meri had questioned Tobi, she'd finally sighed, "Well, they had played with me earlier and wouldn't let me come. Said it was part of my kazillion punishment points from when I was pregnant. Can you believe they actually kept a list? A fucking tally? Unbelievable. Who has time for that shit? Anyway, I was plotting their demise and Peter sold me out like a two-dollar date. Don't let those pretty green eyes fool you, he's a minion for the demons."

Meri couldn't help smile as she remembered the dancing light in Tobi's eyes as she'd recounted the spanking she'd gotten on the club's main stage. Evidently Kent and Kyle had decided to give a lesson on the importance of "transparency" and used their lovely submissive as an example. Tobi had still been sitting on a large pillow as she'd told the story during one of their girls' night-in parties. None of them had gotten to hear the end of the tale because they had all been hustled back inside when the security feeds had shown a boat anchored close to the Prairie Winds' small dock. Meri still shuddered each time she thought about how frightened Regi had been the night she swore she'd seen her dad on a boat out in the river.

Regi had believed for years her parents had been murdered, only to find out they'd faked everything in order to disappear. And within minutes of *finding* her father again, she'd watched as he'd been sucked into the abyss off the coast of Belize—or so she'd believed until she'd seen him standing on the deck of a boat. Meri wasn't sure the Doms at Prairie Winds were convinced he'd survived, but they *were* convinced *Regi* believed it, and that was all that was needed to drop a net over all the submissives they considered *theirs*. Even though Regi had been the last to forgive Meri for her involvement in the incident with Tobi at the club, they had since become good friends.

The night of Tobi's very public spanking, Meri had been in the dungeon with Masters Ash and Dex providing them all some much needed stress relief. It was the last time she'd been at the club and she leaned her forehead against the glass of the dining room window as she thought back on that night. Closing her eyes and taking a deep breath, Meri felt herself tumbling headlong into the memory. She'd had a particularly difficult day at work and somehow they had sensed the desperation she was feeling to get out of her own head.

Ash had stood back from her with his legs spread and his arms crossed over his chest. The well-worn leather pants he'd worn outlined his rigid length in a mouthwatering display that had drawn her eyes despite his order to keep her gaze on the floor as she stripped. She'd seen a muscle flex in his jaw and she wondered briefly if he'd tried to hide a smile of satisfaction before he'd said, "If you want my cock, pet, you are going to have to earn it. Now turn around." He'd stepped up behind her and finger combed her hair before working it into a loose braid. She'd been surprised at the ease with which he'd handled the task and he'd chuckled. "I can almost hear the questions bouncing around it that pretty little head of yours, pet. Ask me what you want to know and maybe I'll answer you."

"Where did you learn to braid hair, Sir? You did it so perfectly."

"Very nice, pet. I have several nieces who have long hair. I learned to braid because it was much less difficult than detangling. And as for perfectly—well, I have to admit it's much easier to do when the subject is standing still." She hadn't even realized he'd been slowly backing her toward the large St. Andrew's Cross until the textured wood pressed between her shoulder blades. She'd gasped and he'd smiled with a glint in his eyes that warned he wasn't really happy. Turning her, he spoke against her ear as Ash tightened the straps at her wrists and ankles, tethering her to the cross. "If you belonged to us, we'd paddle that great ass of yours each and every time you weren't aware enough of your surroundings to know someone was moving you." She'd felt her body respond to his words and he'd reached forward to slide his fingers through her quickly dampening folds. "I do love the way you respond, pet. So wet. Your smooth pussy lips swelling and opening like a rose as your body prepares itself for us. Beautiful."

He pushed a finger deep inside and moved the calloused tip forward until it brushed ever so temptingly against the magic spot that was sure to send her over. Even now she could almost hear her gasp and feel the shudder of surrender that had shaken her all the way to her core. "Not yet, you haven't earned an orgasm yet, pet."

"Please, Sir. I'm so...so close. I don't know how long I can...hold it. Oh God in heaven, please I can't...it feels so good." She'd been sure she was going to burst into flames even though she had only rarely been able to come without pain. Just when she felt her knees were about to fold, he'd pulled his fingers from her and pushed the slick digit between her lips at the same time Dex had spanked her. The blow from his hand had stung, but it hadn't been enough to push her the rest of the way over. By the time they'd finished securing her to the cross she felt herself letting go. Her mind had already started switching gears and Meri loved the feeling of freedom that submission gave her.

Suddenly she felt herself pulled back against a rock hard chest and felt Ash's warm breath against her ear. "What did I tell you the last time you weren't cognizant of your surroundings? And your need for caution is even more important now." When she didn't immediately answer, he reached down and slid his hand up the inside of her thigh. "Answer me, pet, before I decide to deal with this before your sweet housekeeper is even out of the house."

That threat brought her back from her memories and she finally managed to stutter out, "You warned me you would spank me...but this is my home, I'm supposed to be able to let my mind rest here."

"You can only let your mind *fully let go* when you are with Master Dex or myself, no matter where you are." His voice lacked the hard edge she'd heard in it earlier, and his obvious concern for her safety was easy to hear. "Now, Miss Hattie has just been escorted to her car. She said she would be back on Monday at ten-ish, whatever the fuck that means. And Masters' Carl and Peter are going to make another round to secure the perimeter before coming back inside." Her entire body had shuddered at the thought of all four of them inside her home.

At Prairie Winds she'd already noticed it didn't matter how large the room, it would shrink exponentially when more than one SEAL entered the space. So knowing they were all four going to be in her home was daunting. She started trying to work out where everyone was going to sleep when Ash's fingers found her nipples and pinched them both firmly. Even through her clothing the harsh pinch made her squeak. But it refocused her attention on the man holding her tightly against the hard length of his cock and she didn't doubt that had been his intent. "Where is your mind supposed to be, pet?"

"On pleasing you, Sir...you and Master Dex." Her words sounded strained even to her own ears and she knew he'd hear every bit of the desperate need now coursing through her. One of the things she'd learned quickly was how incredibly gifted Dominants were at reading the body language of the submissives they were playing with. Even those who weren't involved in long-term relationships seemed to rarely misinterpret a sub's response. She'd heard of very few instances where a Dom hadn't handled a scene well. Oh, she knew it happened, but that was why there were strict rules about safe words and the dungeon monitors continually monitored the activities in all areas of the club.

She had visited other clubs during her travels, but she'd never played in them because she'd never felt safe. Meri had mentioned that fact one night after sharing several glasses of wine with Tobi and Gracie, and both women had immediately hushed her and warned her not to say anything like that unless she wanted it getting back to Kent and Kyle. Their words of warning had been too little, too late because Kyle had given her a stern lecture about visiting *any* club alone before he'd put her into the taxi he'd summoned for her. She'd been tipsy enough that she hadn't intended to drive home, but that hadn't kept her from frowning about his high-handed treatment. Her car had been parked in the drive the next morning and her keys laying on the front entry table. When she called Tobi to ask how they'd gotten in, her friend had laughed at her, "Locks only keep mortals out...they don't mean anything to SEALs."

"Are you boring her or is she just that distracted?" Dex's words brought her back to the moment just before she heard Ash growl behind her.

"Pet, you are just determined to stretch the limits of my charming personality to its very limit today, aren't you?" Even as distracted as she'd been, Meri didn't miss the underlying message. His tone had been a dangerous mix of sarcasm and warning with just a touch of amusement that she doubted was even close to enough to save her from the coming *reminder* of how important it was to stay in the moment. If she was being honest with herself, she'd admit that when a scene first started it usually took both Ash and Dex to get her focused solely on what was happening at that moment. Once the scene was in full swing they'd often dealt with her one-on-one, but she was self-aware enough to know it was the initial switching of gears that gave her so much trouble. Unfortunately, there seemed to be a big difference between recognizing the problem and fixing it.

I really need to work on my focus, I'll call Dan and ask him if he knows some miracle cure for it. Oh who am I kidding, I've been like this since I was a kid. My old room in Mom and Dad's wing would probably work well for Carl. And the blue guest room will suit Peter. Oh, I hope Tony picked up my blue dress from the dry cleaner. I'm going to pack it last and hope it doesn't get too wrinkled before the gala. Damn it, I think I left the tickets on my desk.

DEX STOOD IN front of Meri watching as she worried her bottom lip. He could almost hear the wheels of her mind spinning. His oldest sister had always been completely focused, but he'd often seen the same completely disconnected look in his sister, Sarah's, eyes. She was less than a year older than Dex, so they'd spent a lot of time together as kids and he had asked her once where she went during the times she seemed "unplugged" from her surroundings. She'd grinned and proceeded to map out her latest mental road trip. He remembered being completely stunned at how each thought had seemed to ping her mind in a new direction. She'd compared it to mental scavenger hunt, where each discovery was a clue that sent you in search of the next random piece of the puzzle. The one thing his sister had said that had burned into his memory was that she often dreamed of being able to escape the "noise" in her head. She'd laughed and said all those thoughts bouncing around in her head were loud, and she wished she knew how to quiet it all down.

He'd seen that same look in Meri's eyes a couple of times at the club, but when he and Ash had worked together they'd been able to quickly focus her attention.

Dex found it interesting that Ash's touch alone wasn't working—it was something he and Ash needed to discuss. If he was right, they would be able to provide that brilliant mind of hers with relief a lot more effectively until they had a chance to condition her responses to them as individuals. Until then, they needed to work together to keep her safe and bind her to them. Dex had grown tired of waiting for Ash to make a decision about Meri. He knew his friend as well as he knew himself, and didn't doubt she was perfect for them, but Ash still hadn't let go of his anger at Catina's betrayal. Dex hadn't ever met the woman Ash had caught in bed with his college roommate, but he'd seen the fire burn in Ash's eyes anytime the subject came up.

Dex knew a couple of his girlfriends had cheated while he'd been away on missions. SEALs and their significant others were a tight group, so keeping secrets was almost impossible. But he hadn't taken their infidelity personally. Actually he considered it their character flaw, not his, and he'd simply walked away. But something about Ash's situation had left a deep gaping wound that never seemed to quite heal. Dex hoped his friend got it resolved before he managed to fuck up things with Merilee Lanham, because since the moment he'd first seen her, his mind had been screaming "Mine!"

Dex leaned forward and kissed the tip of Meri's nose before flashing her what his granny had always called his Snidely Whiplash smile. "Let's get this sweet subbie's punishment taken care of so we can fuck her, what do you say, Master Ash?" He might have been talking to his friend, but Dex hadn't taken his eyes off hers. Not wanting to miss the way her pupils dilated when she knew there was pain in her immediate future didn't affect him as much as it did

Ash, but it was still a hell of a motivator. Her breathing was faster and the pulse pounding at the base of her throat told Dex everything was still on track.

The wide wooden paddle he'd chosen from the bag in his truck was made of maple and would bring the blood to the surface quickly, sensitizing her with each stinging swat. But it wouldn't be enough to give her the burn she needed to really let go. He and Ash had gotten in the habit of betting silently how many strokes of Ash's single-tail or belt it would take before Meri floated happily into sub-space, but today wasn't about that. Today was about punishment and reminding her that she not only didn't have to face everything alone, she wasn't supposed to. They might not have made a formal commitment to her, but he was certain Meri knew she'd made a huge mistake.

Dex sensed Ash's hesitance but he wasn't going to let him back down, Meri needed both of them. She enjoyed the lighter side of BDSM she found with him, but she also craved the darker elements that she'd come to expect from Ash. He'd be having a serious heart-to-heart discussion with Ash in the near future, but in this moment there was only one person he planned to focus on and that was the beauty standing in front of him.

Chapter Eight

ASH STEPPED BACK and let Dex take the lead during the first part of Meri's punishment. He'd notice Dex's gaze flick to him several times and knew his friend had picked up on his trepidation. Sometimes the man was more intuitive than was convenient. Ash moved just enough to the side that Meri would be able to see him remove his belt before she was bent over the table. There wasn't any question about the fact she had more than earned what was coming and her body language told him that she knew it as well.

"Do you have on panties, sweetness?" Dex hated panties with a passion that amused all of the other Doms at the club. Ash had seen him reject unattached subs in clubs all over the world simply because they'd been wearing panties. Ash smiled when Meri's barely audible answer caused Dex's brows to pull together. "I'm fairly sure I've made my view of those offensive garments very clear. And don't give me that bullshit excuse that you didn't know you were going to see us when you got dressed this morning. First of all, I hate them *all of the time,* not just when you are with us. So for the time we're together, you will not wear them unless Master Ash or I give you specific permission to do so. And secondly, we have been together for several hours. Your first and best opportunity to remedy this problem was as soon as we got out of the truck

79

up on the hill."

Ash's cock was instantly rock hard just thinking about Meri stepping from the truck and immediately pulling up the prim skirt she was wearing and stepping out of whatever lace and elastic concoction she had on. There was a small part of him that hoped she made this mistake often because watching her slide little scraps of silk down her well-toned legs would be something to look forward to. Ash looked at Meri with a cocked brow, "Tell me exactly what you think Master Dex thinks you should have done, pet." He'd suspected Meri hadn't really taken Dex's warning seriously, and the pink that flooded her sweet face confirmed his suspicion.

"Well, I guess he wanted me to tell him I had on panties and—"

Dex quickly interrupted her, "No, that is not what I meant at all." Ash had to bite the inside of his cheeks to keep from smiling because Dex's sharp tone had obviously surprised her. "You should have slid that delicious little ass of yours out of the truck and immediately pulled your skirt up and removed your panties. And that is exactly what we'll expect in the future. You'll then hand them to one of us, hanging them from one finger. Do not hide them or your spanking will occur right then and there." Even though she was still fully dressed, Ash could smell her arousal and it was a temptation he was already battling, he had no idea how he was going to finish the scene.

"Now, pull your skirt up around your waist and push your panties down to your knees. If you are going to behave like a bratty girl, that's how we're going to handle you." Ash watched her do as Dex had directed, he wanted to pump his fist in the air when he saw all the moisture in the crotch of her silk thong. "Bend over the table and grab the edge. I'm going to spank you for your deplorable disrespect of Master Jax at the hospital. He isn't your Master, but he is still a Master at the club and you know better than the way you acted. This is meant as a teachable lesson and it is punishment. You are not allowed to come, but I won't gag you unless you are rude." Ash watched as Dex took an unusually hard stance with Meri, he knew if she hadn't had on panties this portion of the punishment would have gone much easier for her.

Dex adjusted her position and rubbed his hand over the smooth skin of her ass and Ash could hardly wait to watch it change from lightly tanned to scarlet. He knew by the time they were finished, the skin would have moved through all the shades of pink and rose before turning a brilliant shade of crimson. Hell's fire would be burning over her ass by the time they'd finished, but he knew she needed this as much as they did. He and Dex had to believe she would come to them the next time she had a problem, and she needed the reassurance that they cared enough to push the issue.

The first blow had been solid and had lifted Meri up on to her toes. "Remember, your safe word will always work, no matter where we are, sweetheart. But I don't think you'll need it, because you need this too, don't you?" Dex's question had ended with two more hard smacks. Meri had closed her eyes trying to lose herself in the pleasure, but neither of them were going to let her go that easily.

"Open your eyes, pet. Keep them on me while you take the punishment you have more than earned." Ash hadn't meant for his words to sound as hard as he knew they had, but he was already battling for his own control. Her eyes opened slowly and were quickly filling with the dreamy distance that told him her mind was already transforming the pain into pleasure. He'd met several masochists over the years, but he'd never met one that could float into the mindset as quickly as Meri once they managed to get her focused. She was the type of submissive every sadist dreams of, yet fears the most.

When Dex had finished, Meri's skin was bright red and her tears had puddled on the table under her pretty face. Dex was speaking to her in soft tones, and Ash knew from experience his friend had pushed Meri, but not nearly far enough to get her where she needed to be in order to find the cleansing release she was seeking. Her eyes went wide and almost glittered in anticipation when he started folding the belt he held in his hands. Watching her, he asked, "Every time you look at this table you see the *gift* your intruder left, don't you, pet?"

Ash wanted to laugh at the startled expression on her face. It wasn't unusual for Dex to make insightful observations during a scene, but Ash usually kept himself firmly in his role as the sadist Dom. It took her a couple of seconds, but she finally whispered, "Yes, Sir."

"Let's see if we can't replace that memory with something else, shall we? The next time you walk into this room, you'll look at this beautiful table and the memory will be of laying over it with your bare ass presented to your Doms for punishment as their friends looked on." *Aha, I didn't think you were aware of our audience.* Even though she had a spectacular body, Merilee Lanham was like most women in her lack of confidence. She didn't realize that her curves, the lush hips, nipped in waist, and softly rounded breasts were what evolution had programed the male brain to pursue.

When she unconsciously started to slide her legs together and stand, Dex's palm in the middle of her back kept her in place. "Stay right where you are, sweetheart, or you're going to earn another punishment."

Meri frozen in place and Ash tilted his head to the side and watched her toes slowly uncurl against the cool tile, and he wanted to smile at the cotton candy pink color of her toenail polish. Panties had always been Dex's issue, but shoes were what Ash wanted his sub to forego. There was a vulnerability about being barefoot, and Ash had long ago noticed the feeling seemed to be especially true with the more hardcore submissives. Even if they weren't consciously aware of it, the message was still there and was rarely missed. She slid her feet back to their original position and Ash watched as her breathing slowly returned to normal. He just continued studying her, noting every shiver and nervous twitch until she finally seemed to let go and let her mind relax. Returning his gaze to hers, he felt like he could fall into the bright green orbs. It was as if he'd fallen into the cool azure water off the coast of Aruba and he found himself surrounded by the unusual color all the time he fought his way back to the surface. He'd never seen a woman whose thoughts were so clearly written in her face. Reading her need to please, he pushed back his body's demand for immediate satisfaction and moved his hand to his supple leather belt and let is slowly slide over his palm.

"When this is finished, I'm going to make you something to eat. We won't be tending the stripes you'll have because you need to feel their burn and the soreness they'll bring for several days. This is a punishment, pet, and we want you to learn from it. But tomorrow, when you look at this table, your pussy is going to slicken at this new memory." Meri's eyes flashed for just a brief moment of trepidation and he was pleased to see even that small bit of survival instinct, because quite frankly they were all too rare.

Moving back behind her, Ash frowned at the deep bruising he already saw starting to show. Looking up at Dex, Ash wasn't surprised to see the stricken look on his face. Folding the belt in half rather that leaving the tail out would help moderate the damage, but there wasn't much more he could do at this point unless Meri used her safe word—and he knew there wasn't a chance in hell that would happen. The first strike surprised her. She yelped and moved, but quickly corrected her position and whispered, "Sorry, Sir."

By the fourth lash he saw the tears begin to subside and after the seventh lash her eyes were unfocused and she'd clearly vacated that busy mind of hers. The next two were harsh—not because he'd wanted to, but she needed the extra push to go over. Just as he swung the tenth strike, he demanded, "Come for me, pet." He dropped the belt, letting it clatter against the floor as he slid his fingers through the soaking folds of her pussy lips. With pinpoint accuracy he pressed against her G-spot and felt the rush of her sweet cream over his fingers as she screamed their names. The convulsing of her vaginal muscles as they locked around his fingers pushed his tenuous control to its very limit. The feel of her silky fluids sliding through his fingers as they were pushed from her core brought on a tightness in his chest that felt like a steel band closing around his heart, anchoring him to her.

DEX WATCHED EVERYTHING play out in front of him and felt as if he was being pulled by some magnetic force into the scene. There was a depth to this moment that he hadn't even realized was missing when they'd previously played with her. And even though it was supposed to have been all about punishment, she'd taken everything they had given her with such grace that Dex had seen the moment Ash's focus snapped, he hadn't fucked her, but he'd given her the release her body was burning for and they'd all found pleasure in the moment. For several seconds, Dex stood stone still—willing his body back from the edge. He hadn't lost control and come from a visual alone since he'd been fifteen, and he certainly didn't plan to do it front of the woman who was fast becoming the center of his world.

When he finally decided his legs might actually hold him up if he took a step, Dex turned toward the kitchen to get a damp towel and came face to face with Peter Weston. Peter simply smiled and handed him the cool, damp cloth he needed. *Damn empaths, always just a step or two ahead of you.* Peter smiled shyly and shrugged in acknowledgment of Dex's thoughts. *Christ, I feel sorry for the women he tops.* Dex grinned at his friends as Peter and Carl stepped quietly from the room to give them a few minutes alone with Meri.

They finished stripping her and then cleaned her with the soft cloth. Dex smiled as goose bumps raced over her dewy skin. "Exhausted, but still so responsive. Come on, let's get you settled while Master Ash makes you something to eat. You'll kneel in the corner of the kitchen and wait." He saw her eyes flare for just a second before she banked the emotion. He was betting she was worried about kneeling on the ceramic tile floor, she hadn't seen the large pillow he'd placed there earlier.

As he helped her into position, his hand skimmed over the burning skin and he heard her moan. He gave her ass cheek a small squeeze, a move that would have brought a yelp from most subs and a scream of pain from many, but Meri simply groaned softly as her body absorbed the sensation. Her mind was still blurring the line between pain and pleasure to the point she was unable to tell any difference between the sensations. Her entire body was flooding with endorphins so her mind would be feeling as if it was free-floating in a pleasurable post-orgasmic state of pure pleasure. The physiology of pain and pleasure was just one of the elements of the lifestyle Dex found most fascinating.

When Dex first started sharing women and scenes with Ash, he'd worried about his friend's more extreme kinks. Dex had struggled to understand how anything but light pain could bring pleasure, and for several months he'd held Ash back while he studied everything he could about masochism. In the end, all the studies, articles, and interviews pointed to one simple truth—it was all about wiring...some people were just wired in a way that let them smudge the line between pain and pleasure until the two were virtually indistinguishable.

It hadn't seemed to matter how many journal articles Dex read or how many expert opinions he sifted through, the information all led to that same conclusion. He'd laughed when he realized one of his old southern granny's favorite sayings was the bottom line it had taken dozens of "experts" years of study to figure out. She might have been lacking "any of those fancy sheep skin diplomas," but she was abundantly blessed with wit and wisdom. Granny had reminded him hundreds of times to "thank your lucky stars not everybody likes the same things, cuz that's what makes the world such a fascinatin' place." *Truer words were never spoken, Granny.*

Chapter Nine

LAYING ON HER stomach on the damned grass wasn't on Trish Jantz's list of most favored ways to spend an evening. She had almost reached the turn off to Ash and Dex's vacant lot when she'd seen Dex's truck pull onto the highway and speed past her. Trish had been practically bouncing in her seat when she'd come upon the accident scene back a mile or so. Seeing the small red sports car crinkled like a tin can and the helicopter waiting to whisk the dying driver away had made her heart sing. After all, everybody knew they didn't airlift out patients unless they were dying, right?

After rigging the slut's car, she'd slipped into a small corner of the hospital's courtyard to watch Ash Moore and Dex Raines. God, they were both so gorgeous she could barely breathe. Hell, she hadn't even wanted to blink for fear they might really be figments of her overactive imagination and vanish before her eyes. Once the program ended, everyone stood and she hadn't been able to see any further than the people immediately in front of her. By the time she'd made her way out of the courtyard, they'd been gone. She'd reached the parking garage just in time to see the little red sports car speeding up the ramp leading to the street. The car's tinted windows prevented her from seeing the driver, but from what the good senator had told her, Merilee Dillon Lanham didn't let anyone else drive her precious automotive gold mine.

Trish had taken her time, stopping at her apartment to shower and change clothes, because she certainly didn't intend to play the sympathetic friend in the soiled clothes she'd worn to crawl under the low clearance car. The oil stain on her shirt and slacks would have been hard to explain, and neither Ash nor Dex ever missed a detail.

When she first met the two Doms two years ago, she'd been a guest at Prairie Winds when they'd been visiting while on leave. They'd played with her, but had kept it light since she hadn't been through the training class. But she'd felt the soul-deep connection and despite their insistence that it was just an introductory scene, she'd known it was just a matter of time before they realized the truth. She'd tried to learn everything she could about the two men, but she had quickly discovered information about Navy SEALs was difficult to come by.

When they had retired and returned to Austin, Trish had *known* they'd come back for her. They had played one night right after their return and it had been perfect. And then that last night they'd been negotiating a scene with her when one of the dungeon monitors interrupted their discussion to tell the men they were needed in the Wests' office upstairs. Before she knew what was happening, Trish found herself cooling her heels in the unattached submissives' area. A half hour later, the unthinkable happened, she'd watched as *her* men stalked through the club's main room leading another woman toward the dungeon. Trish had scrambled to her feet and joined the crowd following the trio and then been furious at what she'd witnessed. It was obvious the scene had started out as a harsh punishment, but it had been equally clear things had changed before everything was through.

Watching Ash and Dex lash the woman would have been an erotic fantasy come true if she hadn't seen the transformation in them midway through the scene. The beginning had given her a unique opportunity to study the dominance styles of both men, information she'd known would be useful in the future. They anticipated one another's moves with an ease born of years of working together. Trish had read a lot about the bonds between SEAL teammates and it had been easy to see that night. She'd gotten so aroused watching them that she'd worried she might climax just standing to the side watching…until she'd seen Dex step up in front of the woman they'd secured to the St. Andrew's Cross. His fingers had moved over the sub's cheek until they were hidden in her long dark hair. The touch had been incredibly intimate and Trish had clearly been able to read his lips when he'd said, "You are doing great, sweetheart."

Trish remembered feeling as if someone had thrown a bucket of cold water over her. Every bit of arousal she'd been feeling had drained away, replaced swiftly with a wave of jealousy to rival the strongest of tsunamis. She had barely been able to watch the rest of the scene, seeing the two Doms known to favor a slightly darker shade of the lifestyle fall under the witch's spell had enraged her. Trish had waited in her small car until the men escorted the woman to her car. Jotting down her license plate number, Trish had then followed the speeding sports car until it had disappeared behind a security gate. The information made it easy to identify Ms. Merilee Dillon Lanham. But the most valuable piece of information had been a small blip in a gossip column mentioning the fact Ms. Lanham and Senator John Stevens had recently stopped keeping company. *Keeping company? Who the hell talks like that besides a pretentious southern gossip goddess?*

Getting a job in Senator Stevens' Austin office had been a piece of cake. Changing her hair color and dressing like Miss Richer-than-God before accidently bumping into him one night at his favorite restaurant had been all it had taken. Getting the asshat to rant about his ex-girlfriend had been easy enough as well, all she'd had to do was endure a few nights of sex so boring she'd worried her mind had actually gone numb.

And tonight, Trish had hoped the men would seek the solitude of their vacant property after losing their beloved piece of ass. She had her story all in place as to why she was there...her poor lost puppy was last seen in this area and she just couldn't bear the thought of him being lost and alone. They'd be able to comfort one another, in her opinion a lost puppy was probably the bigger loss. But looking over and seeing Dex's truck wind its way up the Lanham's drive had surprised her so she'd grabbed her field glasses and cursed when she saw the two men leading the poacher into the house. *Fuck! Who the hell was driving that damned sports car? That nitwit Stevens said she never lets anybody else drive her car. What a dumb bastard.*

MERILEE HADN'T BEEN sure she was going to be able to get through the punishment. It didn't matter how badly she'd needed the physical release, it had been the emotional part that she'd worried might elude her. But she should have known better than to worry, because both Doms seemed to sense what she needed—just as they had every time she'd played with them. With something close to frightening accuracy, Ash and Dex could hone in on her feelings, sense her limits, and then proceed to steamroll right over every single boundary she thought she had and every wall she'd erected in her mind and around her heart.

Her reaction when she'd heard the other men had joined them had been purely reflex, because she simply wasn't accustomed to being bent over her mother's teak dining room table with her ass bared to the world. The wall of windows in front of her had been a continual reminder that they weren't at Prairie Winds but their nearest neighbors hadn't yet built on the hill overlooking the mansion, so she felt confident her stalker hadn't been privy to her punishment. As she knelt in the corner, she let her mind drift over the different things that had happened since her problems started. She was typically a detail person—rarely missing even the slightest variance in things, but she knew she was missing something in this situation and for the life of her she couldn't figure out what it was.

It was times like these that she missed her dad the most. They often brainstormed together. He was one of the most open-minded people she knew, and their late night sessions tossing ideas back and forth had refined more than one major project. She hadn't even realized she was crying until Dex lifted her in to his arms and started up the stairs. "I don't know where you drifted off to, sweetness, but that wasn't where we needed you to be. Let's get you cleaned up before you eat."

DEX HAD SEEN Meri weaving as she knelt in the kitchen and had been watching her closely. When he'd looked up to see Peter frowning in her direction, he'd moved closer. Peter had given him a quick signal for "too far" and even though it was cryptic, he'd known exactly what his friend had been trying to say. She'd had a busy and stressful day and they'd pushed her to the edge in their efforts to get her out of her head for a bit, but in the end he wasn't sure it had worked out as well as they'd planned, and he wasn't sure why.

As he settled Meri in the deep bath and added lavender Epson salts, he'd warned her to stay put until he returned for her and then gone back downstairs. Stepping into the large kitchen, Dex heard Peter explain, "You didn't do anything wrong, Ash. She had a hell of a day, so you have to understand why she didn't fully connect. And for what it's worth, I think she is wondering the same thing and when she has a chance to process it, she is going to feel like she's failed you. That woman is brilliant and driven, but she is submissive to the core. I doubt there is another sub at the club whose submission is as hard-wired into their personality as it is in Meri's."

Dex had grabbed a couple of beers from the bar as he'd walked by, draining the first bottle and quickly opening the second. "Suggestions? I know you were listening, any insight you're willing to share?" All the SEALs that had worked with Peter Weston knew he had very rigid ideas about what was appropriate use of his gift. Dex was hoping Peter would see the information as helping Meri rather than spying on her, but he knew it was likely a matter of perspective.

Ash continued working at the opposite side of the large kitchen, but Dex knew his friend was keeping very close tabs on the conversation. His eyes continually moved to Peter as if he could will their friend to spill the beans. Peter finally sighed and took a deep breath before speaking, "Listen, this is dicey because technically what you asked isn't something I'd usually answer, but if you are going to keep her safe you need to know where her head is…*damn I hate this*. I think she'll tell you exactly what you want to know if you ask her in a way that assures her you aren't disappointed with her. She will shut down on you if you make that mistake. Remember, she has impossibly high expectations for herself, and that is in addition to the fact she will make her Master the absolute center of her universe. Those two things are going to be at odds a lot and any Dom topping Meri needs to be aware that she'll give until there is nothing left if he lets her."

Dex, Ash, and Carl all waited because they all knew Peter's tells and he wasn't finished yet, he was simply rolling his next words around in his mind until he felt they were just right. It was one of the things that had earned Peter the respect of every teammate he'd ever worked with—he didn't speak unless he had something worthwhile to contribute. And he didn't say anything unless it was "ready to be said," Dex held back his smile at the words he'd heard more than once. Peter rolled the glass of ice water he was holding around on the countertop for several seconds, making connecting circles that were starting to remind Dex of a tightly coiled spring, before finally looking up again.

"One of the ways Meri processes information is brain-storming. She does that with her dad and it works for her because he *listens*. Well, more accurately he actively listens."

"Explain." Ash's one word comment showed how out of his element he felt and the fact he cared enough about Meri to even ask gave Dex hope that his friend was falling for her too. *Her too?* The sudden realization that he really had fallen in love with Meri startled Dex enough that he nearly missed Peter's answer.

"I mean that he doesn't try to solve things for her unless she asks him too. I'm not surprised she and Tobi West are close friends because this is one of Tobi's favorite tools as well. These women willingly throw every idea they have out on the table during a discussion. What's more, they don't take it personally when an idea is rejected, because it's all about the process for them. They need to bounce the ideas around and they do that verbally. Think of it as a stone being polished by fine sand. The rock is the basic plan and the sand is all the details, each grain of sand holds an idea, and whether or not it ends up being instrumental in the end isn't important. The real reason it works is because they don't outright reject anything, they see each grain as a piece of the whole." He took a long breath before blowing it out and sighing, "The key to dealing with them is to let them talk through it, ask intelligent, probing questions, and above all, listen to the answers."

Peter paused for a minute and then smiled, "Listen, you guys have been doing this exact same thing for years with your teammates. It's the same concept, but it won't usually involve helos, fast roping, or C4. That last part is kind of a shame, really, but there you have it."

They heard a snort of laughter from behind them and all turned to see a beautiful and completely naked woman standing in the doorway. She was holding a silk robe in her hand but she had known better than to put it on and that pleased Dex way more than it probably should have. "I know I was supposed to wait, but the water got cold and I...well, I could smell the food and I'm really hungry." All four of them were staring at her with their mouths hanging open. Dex knew she had misinterpreted their lack of verbal response when embarrassment and hurt flashed in her eyes for just a second before she looked down and took a half step back. "I'll just go back up and—"

"Stop!" Ash's command had been stern but hadn't sounded threatening, and Dex watched as Meri's nipples immediately puckered into beautiful tight peaks. "I'm glad you came down, and I'm even more pleased that you knew you shouldn't put on anything one of us hadn't given you. And as pleased as I am to see your beautiful curves, I think you'll be more comfortable eating with the four of us if you can wear that pretty robe."

"That doesn't mean you'll get to keep it all evening, because we'd like to start getting you past the body image issue we've sensed on several occasions, but while we eat and work through a few things, we want your entire focus on what we're talking about." Dex's words seemed to settle her, and she looked up and nodded. Since Carl was the closet to her, he took the short midnight blue garment from her hand, holding it open for her. He leaned down and whispered something in her ear that Dex didn't hear, and Ash's growl told him everything he needed to know.

"Lighten up, Ash, for Christ's sake, I just told her that she is beautiful."

"And?" Ash was still glaring at Carl who was obviously enjoying himself.

"Well, yeah. I might have mentioned something about my mild curiosity about what she sees in you two bone-heads, but mostly it was about the fact she is gorgeous and *usually* really smart." Meri giggled and Dex suspected Carl's antics had been intended to break the ice. Carl Phillips had a happy-go-lucky attitude that he used like a shield. All of his teammates had wondered over the years what it was the man was working so hard to hold back. *Not sure I want to be around when that volcano blows, likely to be some mighty powerful stuff.*

Chapter Ten

ACING IN FRONT of the windows of his office, John Stevens was so lost in thought he hadn't even heard Trac Hughes door open, nor had he noticed he was no longer alone. "Not paying attention to your surroundings will get you killed, Senator. And believe me, it's those nearest you that are often the most treacherous." John Stevens might be one of the youngest Senators in U.S. history, but he prided himself on the fact he was as much a predator as any of his colleagues. He had recently been compared to the most treacherous men to ever hold the office, and whether that was a blessing or a curse depended on the circumstance. On the one hand it made fundraising more difficult, but on the other it tended to make his enemies think twice before crossing him.

Senator Stevens spun on his heel to stare at the man charged with keeping him safe. "Well that is what I pay you for if I'm not mistaken? Have you gotten everything in place for that special project we talked about?" People never ceased to amaze him, even though Trac Hughes had come highly recommended by several sources who had raved about his honesty, he didn't seem all that bright in John's view. And after all, honesty was highly overrated, and in John's experience everybody was *ethical,* only until the price was right. And when the money was to their liking, they were just like any other bottom feeder.

Breaking up with Merilee had been a knee-jerk reaction, but damn if Ms. Prim & Proper hadn't blindsided him. John considered himself an excellent judge of character and people rarely surprised him—but she certainly had. He had only been back from Washington a couple of weeks when everything had gone from sugar to shit in a matter of a few minutes. Christ, he'd known their sex was hit and miss, but he certainly hadn't seen it as the dismal failure she'd described. He'd been seething by the time she'd gotten to the fucking point. *Why do women think they have to wax poetic about crap? Just spit it out already.* When she'd finally admitted her interest in BDSM, he'd released the tenuous hold he had on his impatience and lashed her with words that would have made a two-bit hooker blush.

Hell, he'd known how much his words had hurt her, it had been written all over her face. He'd expected tears and apologies, after all she was a Southern Lady to her core. What he hadn't expected was her to nod politely before saying, "I see. Well, then I guess that's that. Thank you for our time together. I wish you every happiness and success. Goodbye, John." And like a dumbass, he'd stood stock-still with his mouth hanging open and watched her walk out. The soft snick of the latch of his condo's front door had been almost deafening.

John knew he hadn't been in love with Merilee—he doubted he was capable of loving anyone. But for the most part he had enjoyed her company, she was gorgeous, knew all the right people, and her family's deep pockets would have been a nice addition to his own personal fortune. And it hadn't taken long for the aftershocks to begin. Evidently Mama and Papa Lanham didn't appreciate having their precious princess's feelings hurt because their friends had started backing out of their funding commitments before the week had ended.

Fuck me, even her career is perfect for a politician's wife. Why the hell does she have to be beaten to get off? What kind of sick shit is that? Maybe if she hadn't been faking it, I might have known she wanted more. That wasn't to say he could have ever managed to play her way, but he could have worked around it. It wasn't that he was a prude, but in his world those games were reserved for women you paid for. And those women never came into contact with the one you married. Sure it was probably chauvinistic, but when in Rome…

TRAC HUGHES LOOKED at the weasel standing in front of him and tried desperately to keep his disgust from showing. He'd been assigned to Stevens when he returned to Austin because word had been circulating that the good senator was looking for help ensuring the silence of a wealthy and well-connected former lover. Why the man was willing to throw away everything to make sure Merilee Lanham didn't tell the world he was a limp dick in the sack was beyond baffling. Their informant hadn't been sure if Senator Stevens intended to kill Merilee or just humiliate her into oblivion, so the young man had wisely backed away and called his contact at the Bureau. Trac leaned against the side of the man's massive desk and wondered if he'd ever met anyone as completely self-absorbed as the man settling into a chair that looked more like a leather king's thrown than an office chair. Personally, Trac thought Ms. Lanham had probably made the best decision of her life, even if it had brought out the crazy in Stevens.

Posing as the newly *purchased* head of the senator's security team put him right where he needed to be, but after the accident involving Ms. Lanham's car yesterday, Trac needed to find out who else was playing. He had often likened undercover work to a game of chess where several people had pieces on the board at the same time. There had been occasions so many stakeholders and players were involved he'd been tempted to tack notecards to the wall in an effort to sort out who was who in the zoo.

"I was working on the last details, but the accident involving her car changes things. I can guarantee you the Wests and the rest of the Prairie Winds team are going to close ranks around Ms. Lanham. I'm sure it has already happened. She is going to be difficult to *manage* now." He let his words trail off, deliberately being vague in hopes Stevens would take the bait and explain exactly what he was expecting in the end. So far the man had only asked Trac to put a tracer on her phone, set up a few cams, and tap into her home security system. He'd even left the damned monkshood on the table the asshat had requested. *Jesus, Joseph, and Mary. How did the man have time to research that piddly-assed shit anyway?*

Trac hadn't made any big effort to hide the cameras he was supposed to place throughout the Lanham house, and he'd been surprised the four former SEALs hadn't found them immediately. But then they'd been pretty distracted by that hot scene in the dining room. Being a Dom himself, Trac had known just how focused the two men administering the punishment had been. Even at a distance, the intensity of the scene had drawn him in. Trac had been glued to the monitor taking in every nuance...every unconscious response, gasp, and moan. The other two Doms who had joined them after completing a sweep of the grounds had been just as drawn in, so perhaps it wasn't a surprise the equipment had gone unnoticed until this morning.

Trac had scrubbed the feed, there was no reason for Mr. Self-Righteous to see something he would completely misinterpret. It didn't take a rocket scientist to figure out why the senator and Ms. Lanham hadn't clicked. Hell, the woman was as submissive as any Trac had ever seen and her need for pain would have likely flipped a switch in the man whose only love was his career. *I can only imagine how that conversation went down. "Hey, I need more...you know....can you beat me or something?" Queue detonation...*

Unfortunately the good senator didn't seem like he wanted to lay his plans out just yet. "I didn't rig the car if that's what you're implying."

"I wasn't implying anything. I was just explaining why things are going to be more complicated now. Perhaps if I knew exactly what you were hoping to achieve, I might be able to help you find a way to get there." Studying Stevens for a few long, silent seconds during which Trac noted the man had very few "tells" and that meant he was either telling the truth or he was a fucking Zen Master...and Trac's money was on the former.

"Are those cameras you planted working?"

"Not now. Keep in mind the men that are guarding Ms. Lanham are former Navy SEALs. America's best don't miss spy cams when they do a security sweep." *Well, they don't miss them as long there isn't a naked woman bent over the table being lashed for not telling anyone she was in trouble.* Oh that hadn't been their excuse, but it had damned well been the reason. "Even if they hadn't found them, we wouldn't be getting anything because they've set up a jammer so the tracer we put on her phone isn't working either." Of course he'd used the most outdated equipment he could get his hands on hoping the SEALs would start questioning what was happening.

"If you weren't responsible for the accident, that means we have another player on the field and we need to find out who that is—sooner rather than later."

Before Stevens could respond a quick rap sounded on the door just a second before one of his admins walked in, "Oh, I'm sorry. I didn't realize you had someone with you, Senator, I didn't see anything on your schedule." Trac stood and even in the spiked heels she was wearing, his six and a half foot frame towered over her. His friends and family had often teased him about scaring little old ladies and small children just for practice, but the odd thing was those were the two groups that seemed completely immune to his best efforts to intimidate them. There were several elderly widows in his neighborhood and they kept him supplied in food and baked goods to the point he'd finally had to add another day to his gym schedule. And he'd made valiant efforts to coerce his nieces and nephews into behaving without any success whatsoever. But the woman standing in front of him lying through her teeth was eyeing him warily. *Interesting.* She looked enough like Merilee Lanham that they might be mistaken for one another at first glance, but this woman's look came off as "trying too hard" where Ms. Lanham's grace was innate.

When he met her gaze he shifted his feet wide and crossed his arms over his chest in a pose every submissive in the world would recognize, and just as he'd suspected it would, her chin dropped and she suddenly became very interested in everything but him. Her body language was screaming sub, but her eyes sent an entirely different message. Trac had been a Dom for a long time and he'd seen women who craved the attention they received during scenes, they loved having a Dom focused solely on seeing to their pleasure, but they were just playing. In many ways they were like any other narcissist.

This woman doesn't understand the first thing about the power exchange, which is the foundation of BDSM. He was willing to bet her view of submission didn't even hold a mention of pleasing her Dom, and everything the woman standing across the room from him did was calculated down to a gnat's ass. She'd never handed over her trust because she probably didn't trust anyone, not even herself. In some ways she and her boss were a match made in heaven. Trac wondered if Stevens had even noticed that he'd attempted to replace Ms. Lanham with a very cheap imitation.

Well, well, well. Things just keep getting more interesting all the time. I'm more than a little curious about Ms. Trish-the-Admin's story, because something about her is flipping all my alarms.

TRISH KNEW THE new security chief was in Senator Steven's office because she'd been in the next room listening to every word they'd said. John Stevens didn't pay any attention to his phone and Trish had learned within the first couple of days in the office how to program his phone so it operated as an open mic to her phone. All she had to do was put on her headset and pretend to be transcribing. She'd heard more than enough to ensure the good senator wouldn't be firing her anytime soon. Hell, she had enough on him and several of his cohorts to guarantee her financial future, and she intended to cash in as soon as she got rid of the bitch who'd stolen her men. Stevens and his new security hot shot had been boring her to distraction with all their dancing around one another in their conversation. She'd had to fight not rolling her eyes at their tedium, but when she'd heard them begin discussing the accident, it had been time to step in.

Trish was grateful she'd had the foresight to prepare something that needed the senator's attention so it had been quick and easy to simply scoop the documents up from the corner of her desk, give a cursory knock, and then step into Senator Dip-Shit's office. But that was the point where everything she'd *planned* came to a screeching halt. She had only seen Trac Hughes once, he'd been down the full length of the corridor and she'd just caught a glimpse of him before he'd moved through the elevator's open doors. She'd noted his height but the intensity of the man she now faced had been diluted...vastly diluted, by the distance. The chill that raced up her spine was a sharp contrast to the heat that flooded her sex. For just an instant she saw interest flare in his eyes, but it faded quickly as his eyes moved over her. He'd seen something that had caused his gaze to shutter and his entire demeanor had shifted. The shift had been subtle, she'd give him that, but it had been there. Her body had reacted despite her best efforts to stifle the response.

Everything about the man screamed authority, and in the back of her mind Trish wondered if he was a cop. But it was the sexual Dominant that was front and center, and that was who she had to deal with at the moment. His stance mirrored that of every Dom at Prairie Winds and his assessment of her had been instant. She could only hope he saw the illusion most men saw, a reasonably attractive submissive, not the calculating woman whose agenda didn't include anyone who didn't cater to her needs. But at the very least she had successfully derailed their conversation about the accident. The less time people around her spent discussing that misstep, the less likely she was to react and draw attention to herself.

Trish had been glad to hear the man driving Merilee Lanham's car hadn't been seriously hurt, after all why risk a homicide charge for someone she didn't care about? The only time she made mistakes was when she rushed and this had been an epic example. Concentrating on the conversation, she tried to tune out the man standing to the side watching her with a focus that made her uncomfortable on several levels.

MARK STEFANO PACED in front of the desk where his laptop sat open, taunting him by displaying the email he'd written and re-written a hundred times. Every time he stalked by his desk the damned thing was still prominently displayed. Despite the fact he knew exactly what he wanted to say, the words never seemed just right once he'd typed them out. Hell, if he wasn't such a damned coward he'd just call his daughter or better yet, suck up his damned pride and show up on her doorstep. But realistically, how many times could he expect her forgiveness? *Fuck me, this is a mess. How could I have let things get so out of control? I've thrown away the only family I have left.* When he and Nalia had first gone into hiding, the pain of losing Regi had been so much more than he'd expected, and then losing Nalia a few months later had sent him over the edge. He'd spent the next several years in a fog that had rarely lifted long enough for him to even acknowledge where he was. Moving between his family's several homes had been his way of avoiding the fact none of them was a real home, because the two women he'd loved beyond measure weren't there.

Instead of reaching out to Regi—the one person who might have been able to pull him back from the precipice, he'd retreated into his own head and wallowed in the grief for the better part of ten years. By the time he'd finally managed to pull himself back together, he'd been so deep in the family business, there hadn't been a way out. Mark had merely dabbled in the drug trade and had avoided the sex-trade end of things entirely, preferring to concentrate on the *acquisition of* antiquities and their very lucrative resale. One of the first things he'd done after his mother died was shut down all their sex business trade. Saying it had been an unpopular decision was a gross understatement, but even his harshest critics had finally agreed when worldwide attention began to force authorities to make at least a cursory effort to curb the booming worldwide sex trade industry. The attention hadn't been Mark's reason, he'd actually been completely repulsed by the things his mother had sanctioned solely by her inattention.

Stepping back up to his desk, he looked down at the screen but didn't re-read the words he'd already read so many times. Taking a deep breath, Mark forced his shaking finger to press the key that sent the message and he prayed it set his future in motion. No matter the response, every hope he held for the future rested in her hands. *More accurately...it all depends on whether or not Regina can find in in her heart to forgive me...again.*

Chapter Eleven

MERI HAD HEARD both Tobi and Gracie rave endlessly about Ash's cooking abilities, but she'd still been completely bowled over by the meal he'd prepared in such a short period of time. It wasn't any secret the staff her mother employed kept the kitchen well stocked, but the basic fare he'd prepared had been delicious because of the special spices and his attention to detail in its preparation and presentation. All four men had stared at her, amused expressions on their faces as she'd cleaned her plate, not once but twice. She'd always had a voracious appetite and truthfully, she should probably be grateful her metabolism seemed to keep her curvy, not round enough to roll faster than she could walk physique.

When she had finally pushed her plate back, Meri looked up and grinned. "That was amazing, thank you. And I just want to say, your cooking lives up to every one of the reverent compliments Tobi and Gracie have given you."

She felt her cheeks heat under their watchful eyes and she was relieved when Ash finally spoke. "Thank you, pet. It was my pleasure, and just so you know, Master Dex is just as good in the kitchen despite what he might tell you. These other two," he nodded his head toward Peter and Carl, "are more likely to take a woman to some sleazy bar for a burger and fries than they are to feed her properly.

And then they wonder why she crashes on them before last call." Meri couldn't hold back her soft chuckle as the other two men groaned.

"That's just wrong, man. You're going to give her the wrong impression about us," Carl complained. "Don't listen to them, Meri, we treat our dates right. We take them out on the town and let them chose their own fare instead of shoving vegetables at them and boring them with nutritional facts and figures. Can you imagine how dull that will be? Just keep that in mind, sweetie—you know, in case you come to your senses about these two."

She didn't answer, choosing instead to simply nod to let him know she'd heard him. They wouldn't let her help clear the table, insisting she gather anything she might need for their coming strategy session and then meet them in her dad's study. When they turned their attention to the task of setting the kitchen to rights, she hurried out of the room hoping a bit of distance would give her time to organize her thoughts. Grabbing her favorite pen and Big Chief tablet, Meri settled into her usual chair tucking her legs beneath her and immediately felt a calm sense of familiarity settle over her.

Yes, this was exactly where she needed to be, she was just about to get back up and get a glass of water when a tanned arm came from behind and settled onto the small table to her right. "Thanks," she said without turning.

She felt the soft press of Dex's lips against her cheek, "You're welcome, sweetness." All four men were in the room, but she noted Carl and Peter had chosen to stay farther back, probably in hopes of lessening her distraction. "Now, tell us how to make this work for you. In order for us to protect you, we need your input. We'll be asking you a lot of questions, so it's important we make the whole process as easy and productive as possible."

Meri felt tears press at the back of her eyes at Dex's sweet words. She appreciated the fact they were making such an effort to seek her input and let her help in the only way she knew how. She also needed a way to work through all the random thoughts bouncing around inside her head and brainstorming was her best bet. When things were happening that she couldn't make sense of, the only way she'd ever been able to sort it through was to play a full-on game of verbal volleyball with her dad. Taking a deep breath, she tried to shift her mind away from the pain brought on by a sudden wave of loneliness.

As Ash settled in her dad's chair, she moved her chair back and encouraged the others to form a semi-circle facing him. Trying to find the door in her mind that let ideas flow, Meri doodled absently on the tablet paper that had always been her favorite. Schools might not use Big Chief tablets as often as they did in the past, but Meri was convinced she was playing a large part in their continued production.

She felt a bit lost because she'd never had to take the lead before, her dad had always asked her a few questions in the beginning and then just let her run. The silence was starting to make her nervous when she felt something shift around her. Damn, she'd forgotten about Peter's gift and when he leaned forward he grinned, "I'm sorry, Meri, but you just think incredibly loud." His soft chuckle relaxed her and she felt her self-consciousness ease a bit. "How about this, I'll ask you a couple of questions and we'll see where it leads. Will that work for you?"

"Yes, please. I just need someone to point me in the direction you want to go." From the very first question, Meri felt herself move into what she'd often referred to as "the zone". Her mom had often teased her that she was like her dad in the way she could narrow her focus with pinpoint precision and completely focus on a task, particularly when it required her to think on several different levels at the same time. She enjoyed the process with these men because individually, she suspected they were all well above average in intelligence, but working together, they were something to behold. She'd often heard about the concept of synergy, but had rarely seen it more clearly exemplified.

THE MINUTE HE'D settled in her father's massive office chair, Ash had seen a subtle change in Meri. It had been as though she had moved onto a familiar place, a well-practiced ritual that required a figure of authority in the chair in front of her. It really shouldn't have surprised him, she was deeply submissive, after all, and most of the hardcore subs he'd met had been incredibly responsive to formal and predictable practices. He found it interesting that Meri's submission wasn't tied specifically to predictable sexual elements—hers was apparently much broader.

Once again, Peter's help had proven to be solid gold. Ash made a mental note to thank his friend. He and Dex could have probably gotten Meri where she needed to be eventually, but it had certainly been easier with Peter's insight. Ash had been impressed with her ability to step out of the situation and see things from a variety of angles. He'd always considered that ability to be one of the things that distinguished ordinary bright individuals from those that were truly exemplary. It was no doubt something her father had recognized and carefully cultivated over the years as he'd prepared her for her role as the head of the foundation that bore her family name.

While Meri had been upstairs, he'd asked Carl to do a quick bit of research into the Lanham Foundation and the results were damned impressive. The organization's projects were often collaborative efforts because of their broad scope, and their partners were carefully chosen. The assets of the privately held group were staggering and even though they spent monumental amounts of money, their portfolio grew significantly each year. He was enough of a realist to recognize the vast differences in their backgrounds and he worried that he nor Dex would ever fit into her world, for the moment he needed to push those thoughts aside. Right now, keeping Meri safe was his only priority and he'd concentrate on that until they figured out who was responsible for the problems she'd been experiencing.

Carl and Peter's interior sweep had yielded several spycams that they'd all been embarrassed to admit they hadn't seen earlier. Either the antique units had been purchased at a swap meet by an uninformed amateur or they'd been used deliberately by someone trying to send a message. And the fact whoever had put them in place hadn't made even the barest hint of an effort to hide them had Ash betting someone had been hired to do a job they either didn't agree with or didn't care anything about.

Something was definitely *off* with the entire situation, but Ash wasn't sure exactly what it was. The information she gave them about the earlier incidents didn't fit at all with what had happened when Tony had driven her car. Looking at the other men, he asked, "Something is not right here...do you think we could be dealing with more than one perp?"

Meri's gaze snapped up from the tablet she'd absently

been doodling on and he saw the worry in her eyes. "Do you mean you think there might be two people who want to hurt me? Why? I just can't fathom what I could have done to make any one person that angry, let alone two." He'd heard the desperation and fear in her voice, but he had the feeling the real issue hadn't been fear for her safety. The real problem was she was simply mortified by the idea anyone could be that angry with her, and that was the part he was having the most trouble grasping as well. And from the looks on their faces, the other men were struggling with the same question. Hell, each of them had made enough enemies to last a lifetime and their new positions with the Wests' tactical teams weren't likely to win them legions of fans either, but Meri was an entirely different matter.

Carl recovered first and smiled at her, "Sweetness, we were all stunned for a minute because we've had enemies who wouldn't hesitate to do this and much worse, I assure you. It's a credit to a woman in your position that you don't have a string of enemies for us to sort through…but the flip side of that is, we don't have much to go on."

"There really are only two people who can even be considered as *on the list*." She was twirling the pen through her fingers in an intricate pattern that told him how often she used the motion to help her focus her thinking. "And as we've discussed, I don't believe neither of them really is a viable option. Although John would have more reason to want me to keep quiet. But I have to say I'd sooner suspect him if he was just trying to scare me into running to him for protection."

Ash tilted his head to the side, "Explain that please."

"Well, it wasn't uncommon for him to throw a tantrum about this, that, or the other. For the most part I just ignored him, but it was getting old in a big hurry." *Getting old? What the fuck? Why would she have ever allowed that to occur more than once? Another thing we'll be discussing at length.* Ash was starting to appreciate Kyle and Kent's complaints about Tobi being oblivious to the boundaries she should force others to observe.

"And if you tried to reason with him, or offer any sort of explanation, he would just scream louder. I finally got to the point where I would just walk away. I walked out of his condo downtown one night without my shoes...luckily I'd left my purse by the door. From that point forward I left my shoes there as well."

Ash heard the growl rumble in his chest a split second before he realized he was on his feet and moving around the wooden *structure* her dad called a desk. *Christ, the thing has to be ten feet long and at least five feet wide. Hell, I've seen smaller dance floors in bars.* Once he'd pulled her from her chair he folded his arms around her and pressed her against his chest. He wasn't sure who he had intended to comfort, but it sure was helping them both. The fact she was trembling at the memory of her time with Senator Stevens made Ash want to teach the man what it was like to be intimidated. He might be a sadist during sex play, but Ash had a bone-deep aversion to bullying.

Growing up in the South where the social structure was still largely patriarchal, Ash had seen and heard enough stories of domestic violence to last a lifetime. And he'd known good soldiers who'd made serious mistakes in their relationships simply because they had returned to their families before they'd completely decompressed after missions.

For some reason, Ash had always associated civilian domestic abuse problems with men and women who were either undereducated or poor—and often both. But now, knowing a woman with Merilee Lanham's intelligence and vast financial resources had tolerated—even for a short time—being emotionally and verbally abused changed the way he viewed the problem. Sending up a silent prayer of thanks for the people like his mom who volunteered at their local women's shelter, Ash just held her until he was sure the anger he was feeling wouldn't show in what he wanted to say.

Releasing her, he moved back enough to look down into her eyes, "Did he ever make threats to you? Any kind of threat at all?"

"Not really, he usually just tried to belittle me—make me question my value as a person because that was his way of feeling important, and he thought I'd be more dependent on him. I don't think he wanted me to feel I could function without him. To say he has an overinflated opinion of himself would be an enormous understatement." Meri stepped back and leaned against the desk, hell, the thing was too high for her to scoot up on without jumping. She seemed lost in thought for a few seconds before continuing, "But at his core I think he is insecure, so making me feel bad about myself was his way of ensuring I'd stay. I know it sounds really twisted, but from what I've read, it's really a classic symptom. But…well, that wasn't the way I wanted to live my life, so I walked away. There was no big break-up or anything, I just wished him well, said goodbye, and walked out. So I can see where he might want to frighten me enough to seek him out for protection, especially since I'm sure he knows my parents are gone."

Dex had moved to their side and tipped her chin up so her eyes met his, "Is it possible his behavior could have escalated to the point of wanting to silence you? And would he be willing to slide under your car to attach the device that was used to hold the accelerator down?" They hadn't told her about the timed magnet that was used on her car. It had actually been a pretty sophisticated device, much more so than the cameras they'd found in the house—which was another reason he was leaning toward more than one suspect.

"I just can't see it. First of all, I can't imagine him knowing that much about cars. I don't know what kind of device you're talking about, but he didn't even know he was supposed to have the oil changed in his car, so it probably doesn't matter. He knows a little more about computer hardware, but not much."

"What does he know about?" Ash was starting to wonder what she'd seen in the man.

"Well, he's a master at self-promotion. Even though he's an ass in private, in a social situation, he is utterly charming. He studies every detail about the people he *needs* to smooze. He knows their spouses, what they do for a living, their kids' names and ages. I've seen him recall the scores of a ball game one of his largest contributor's son played in. Using that kind of information when you are soliciting campaign funds and political support is very powerful stuff. He remembers some things, but mostly he studies continually.

"He went to college in the northeast and was on a rowing team. He also loves to sail, but doesn't get to do that very often now although he does keep a boat out on the lake." Ash watched as Meri wrinkled her brow, he knew she was searching her mind for something—anything that would help them, but the fine lines at the corners of her eyes betrayed the exhaustion that was quickly fogging her thinking.

Turning toward the other two men, Ash spoke softly, "You two update Micah, he's running scenarios through his system, and then take the first two watches. Text our phones when it's time to switch out and we'll relieve you."

Carl and Peter both stood and turned toward the door, "Thank you." All four of them looked at her curiously. Her posture straightened and Ash got a glimpse of the *suck-it-up and be gracious no matter what* Southern woman he'd known was inside her. He had to fight back the grin, and he could tell Dex was doing the same. "I know I didn't thank you all for helping me, but it's important that you know how grateful I am that you're here. It was frightening to know that someone was in the house while I was upstairs that night."

Both men smiled and nodded before heading to the door, but just as he was about to step out of the room, Peter turned back to her and grinned, "Sweetie, learning to handle and fire a weapon is a great idea, but I think you'd be much wiser to ask your men for help rather than Lilly West. From what I hear, Lilly has a tendency to *over-do* things a bit." Ash felt himself blanch at Peter's comment and the stricken look on Dex's face let him know his partner was just as mortified.

Chapter Twelve

THE NEXT FEW days were a blur. Meri often found herself surrounded by men she'd only seen at the Prairie Winds Club, and having so many people in and around her home was often daunting. Even though they were much more relaxed away from the club, there was never any doubt that each and every one of them was a Dominant. It had taken her a couple of days to grasp the fact that as long as she stayed out of the way, things seemed to run smoothly and they spoke openly in front of her. She leaned against the wall of floor to ceiling bookshelves in her dad's office and listened to them discuss the significance of the spy cams they'd found. She'd heard this same discussion time and again and wondered why it was an issue.

"I made some calls and from what I'm hearing, the good senator is almost continually under investigation. But the scuttlebutt is that he's gotten a new chief of security since he returned to town." Kyle opened the folder he was holding and started handing out pictures. "Take a look, I want to know if any of you recognize him."

Jax McDonald was the first to speak, "I've seen him…and recently too. But it may take me a minute or two to remember where. Fuck, I have to get more sleep. If Deaga doesn't start sleeping more, I swear I'm going to override Gracie on the nanny issue." Meri was holding back her giggle when he suddenly seemed to remember she was in the room, "Sorry about the language, Meri. My mama would have my head if she heard me say that in front of a lady."

"Your secret is safe with me, Jax. And for what it's worth, I think it just shows how exhausted you are. I also don't think Gracie is as opposed to a part-time nanny as she was earlier, so you might want to bring the subject up again."

"Thanks, I'll do that. And if she agrees, Micah and I will owe you one. A big one."

Meri stepped forward to look down at the picture and gasped, "I know him. I saw him two years ago at an event. I doubt he'll remember, because we weren't actually introduced, but my dad pointed him out to me. He's with the FBI, or was at that time. There were only a few people in the room I didn't know and he was one of them. His name is Trac Hughes." She suddenly realized all of them were staring at her, "What? Oh, it's the memory thing isn't it? Well, I have a really good memory, there are people who cared enough to test it and then wanted to argue semantics. You know, whether it was eidetic or photographic...like it really makes any difference. Sorry, that was probably more than you wanted to know about that, but anyway, there you have it."

Kent West burst out laughing, "Damn, Merilee. That explains a lot. Please tell me that it isn't contagious or I'm going to have to put an end to yours and Tobi's friendship." His wink told her he was kidding, or at least she hoped so.

"No, I'm fairly sure it's not catching. And I have to admit it isn't always a gift either."

Peter snorted, "Amen to things not always being a

gift," made Meri realize for the first time just how difficult Peter Weston's life had to be at times, and she suddenly found herself seeing him in a whole new light. She saw just the smallest tint of pink color his cheeks as he grinned at her, "Thanks, Meri. Not everyone gets it."

Ash looked around the room, "Well, this might well explain the antique cams, my guess is Agent Hughes was trying to send us a message."

Micah laughed, "Agreed. Hell, even they don't use that stuff anymore. I'd be willing to bet he had a little trouble finding the pieces he used here. I'd say that was a deliberate attempt to get our attention."

Peter nodded in agreement as Carl explained, "He basically set the stuff right out in the open and made it easy to back-trace the signals to Senator Steven's office. Agents don't make those kinds of mistakes. I'd say he wanted us to know what Stevens is up to without directly compromising his investigation."

The room fell silent for a few moments while everyone considered the implications of what they'd learned. But it was Meri who broke the silence, "Has he ever visited the club?" Every man in the room turned toward her as if the movement had been choreographed, but when she realized they each had raised a brow in exactly the same way, she had to resist the urge to roll her eyes. *Yeah, rolling your eyes in a room full of Doms—definitely not a good plan.* "Okay, don't get all testy, here's why I asked...the time I saw him, his body language screamed Dom." When they continued to stare at her with unblinking eyes, she sighed and continued, "Oh come on, you all know exactly what I'm talking about. Anyway, the Prairie Winds Club is the best in or around Austin...heck, it's arguably one of the best clubs in the country, so it stands to reason that he's either visited or would like to. So perhaps you can arrange a *visit* and speak with him there…that way you'll know nothing is being recorded. And your scramblers will prevent anything wireless on his end as well."

The moment she mentioned the scramblers, Meri realized her error but it was too late. *Probably not much chance of the whole lot of them missing that gaffe.* And just as she'd feared, Kyle West growled, "I'm going to beat her ass." Meri took an involuntary step away from him and his face softened, "I wasn't talking about you, sweetie. And you and I both know she is going to like it far too much for it to have any effect on her behavior. Tell me just exactly how this topic came up in a group of ladies who have much more interesting things to discuss than our security protocols." His tone might be mild, but holy Hannah, the man was seriously peeved.

"Well, to be honest, I already suspected, and when Tobi didn't correct my assumption, then I knew for sure. She didn't *tell me*, you know better than that Kyle. And despite your frustration with her, I still admire the fact she wasn't willing to lie. She and I had a rocky start…to say the least, and I'm honored that we've developed a friendship that is based on that kind of honesty."

To his credit, Kyle West had the decency to seem at least a little chastened as Kent came to his rescue, "We'll be asking you more about how you *knew* later, Meri. But for now, I want to move on with your suggestion because we need to wrap this up. But for what it's worth, I'm glad things worked out the way they did between you and Tobi, and she is lucky to count you among her friends." His words sent a surge of warmth straight to her heart and she felt tears press against the back of her eyes. For the first time she felt completely absolved of the sins of that fateful night at the club and she was nearly overwhelmed by the emotion.

Dex watched Meri through the shower's steamed door and grinned. She'd handled the meeting downstairs like a pro. Even if you didn't factor in her submissive nature, the group of former SEALs/Doms she was facing were a force to be reckoned with. As Masters at a BDSM club, they could and often did reduce subs to tears with little more than a look. But Meri had politely countered them when she'd thought they were out of line on security concerns and asked questions he knew were more to provoke conversation than because she needed or wanted the information. In short, he'd been damned impressed, and for some reason that made her even more attractive to him.

"She's amazing isn't she?" Ash's quiet question from the doorway was easy to answer.

"Incredible. I wasn't sure we'd ever find her, you know?"

"I do, and now we just need to keep her safe long enough to convince her to belong to us." Dex nodded in agreement as he stepped out of the room and closed the door quietly behind him.

"There's more than one perp—I'm just sure of it, but I can't get an angle on the second one. And what was that comment Peter made about the weapons? If she wants to learn to shoot, we'll be the ones teaching her. I'm going to have nightmares for weeks thinking about her learning from Lilly West." Dex saw Ash shudder and knew his friend was in agreement. Lilly West was, without any question, one of the most interesting women Dex had ever met. All of Kent and Kyle's teammates had met their mother at one time or another during their years of military service. And he didn't know a single man among them that didn't love Lilly. She was smart, witty, irreverent, loving, and a crack shot. She'd used firepower more than once to defend someone she cared about—there was no doubt she was capable. The only problem was, she tended to follow the philosophy of more is better, and if she had the choice between a fly swatter and a canon to kill a mosquito, the canon was certainly going to be her weapon of choice.

When Dex heard the shower shut off he returned to the enormous bathroom and grinned when Meri stepped out and shrieked, "Holy crapping carp, you scared the life out of me. How did you get in here? I locked the door. I always lock the door. I know I locked it. Geez, listen to me. I'm rambling. I really hate that, but it's because you rattled me. You're lucky I didn't hit you with something. I'm like that when I get scared, I lash out and it's awful. I really hate to be scared."

Realizing how badly he'd startled her, he stepped forward and wrapped his arms around her. "I'm sorry, sweetheart. I had no idea you would be so flustered. And yes, you did lock the door, but, love, that lock is really a joke. If you really want a lock on the door for the times we aren't here, we'll install one, but truthfully, that lock is just lame." When he'd been in the bathroom earlier he'd noticed the panties she'd placed on top of the clothing he assumed she was planning to wear, and the lace and elastic scrap of nothing was now in his pocket. He knew she planned to go to her office for a few hours before they all went to the club, but he and Ash had other plans for her—

and she certainly didn't need panties for what they had setup for her out on the patio.

ASH STEPPED INTO the bathroom in time to hear Dex's words to Meri and wondered what had startled her so badly. But when he looked down at her naked form he lost all focus on the words she and Dex were speaking. *Holy fucking hell!* For several seconds he wasn't even sure he was breathing. He didn't think he'd ever seen the remnants of bruises that particular color. And to know that he and Dex were responsible almost made him physically ill. With a flash of insight, Ash wondered how much worse it had been after her punishment at the club the first night they met.

The fact she'd managed to keep this a secret for the past few days was another issue they'd be discussing at length. But then he remembered that she had in fact mentioned being a "bit sore" and that was why they hadn't pressed for sex. She had been in bed under the covers the past two nights when he'd come in from showering in another bathroom, but damn, this had been far more than a little sore. Sure, it was obvious the deep tissues bruises were healing, but he wondered how the marks had looked a day or two ago. The look on his face must have alerted Dex there was a problem because Ash heard him ask, "Sweetheart, Master Ash is standing behind you and looks like he is about to have a stroke. Want to tell me why or should I just check myself?"

Ash heard her gasp just before she started struggling to step away from Dex, her arm waving frantically in the air trying to snag a towel from the nearby bar. Dex held tight, it was obvious Dex wasn't planning to release her. "Stop." By the time the word registered in Meri's mind, Ash could tell she was nearing panic. *Christ, does she think we're going to add to her bruises?* Even though Ash considered himself a sadist in BDSM play, he wasn't about to injure the woman in his care. The only pain he gave a sub was that which had been agreed upon in advance. And they were definitely going to be renegotiating limits after what he was seeing.

Dex slowly turned Meri until she was facing away from him and Ash saw her tear-filled eyes and Dex's scowl. Ash heard her whisper, "It's not that bad" at the same time he heard Dex's low whistle.

"Not that bad? Are you fucking kidding me? Compared to what? Jesus, I don't even want to think about what this looked like a couple of days ago. And you didn't consider this important information?" Ash heard the rising frustration in Dex's voice and knew his friend well enough to see things were going to be FUBAR in seconds if he didn't intercede. Dex rarely lost his temper, but when he did, it was a flash fire that scorched everything around him.

"Pet, tell me what your ass looked like after your punishment the night we met." Hell, the look on her face alone answered his question. *God you gotta love a sub with such open and honest expressions.* For just a moment he completely lost focus as he took in the incredible sight of her. She was stunning and as genuine as anyone he'd ever met. Whatever you saw reflected in her expression was the absolute truth with her. *I'll bet she is the worst poker player ever.* He wasn't completely sure how it would all play out, but he knew the woman standing in front of him had just rocked his entire world, and she hadn't even really done a thing. But something in her eyes lit a fire in his soul he hadn't even realized had been kindled—just waiting for a special woman to set aflame.

"Well, to tell you the truth it looked pretty awful for a few days. I really hadn't intended to, well, let anyone…umm, you know…"

Dex knew he wasn't going to like the way this story ended, but he wasn't about to let it go either. "No, sweetheart, I'm afraid we don't actually know so you are going to have to enlighten us. And let me remind you that editing is not allowed. Just spit it out. You won't be punished for telling the truth." That wouldn't always be true, but it would be true that punishments for lying were always exponentially more severe.

They both watched as she seemed to consider her words and for once Ash was inclined to give her a few moments to gather her thoughts. He didn't have the impression she was planning to lie, but he could almost feel the tension vibrating through her. *Does she think we'll stop now that we know how badly we've marked her?* Just as he was about to ask her, she looked up at them both, her eyes bright with unshed tears. "My mom walked in on me while I was in the changing room at Chico's and well, she sort of lost it." Ash felt like he'd been gut punched. Not only had they failed her as Doms, now her mother was going to hate them forever. And if her family was anything like his own, her father had been informed as well. *Fucking perfect.*

Chapter Thirteen

DEX SETTLED MERI on his lap in the club's main lounge and smiled at the other Doms sitting in the small circle. Sam McCall had his wife, Jen, settled in a similar position—angled so he had access to her front and back with her legs draped over the outsides of his widespread knees. But Jen was naked and her arms were also bound behind her. Her clit and pretty pink nipples were all clamped and linked with a fine gold chain that Sam kept swirling around his finger and pulling in quick jolts as they talked. Personally, Dex didn't know how much more the poor subbie was going to be able to take before she came without her Master's permission, and he'd bet that was exactly what Sam was hoping for. Her breathy moans were increasing in intensity and a fine sheen of sweat glistened over her skin. "Pet, let me remind you that you do not have permission to come. Your other Master hasn't arrived yet and you heard what he said."

Jen pulled her bottom lip between her teeth and nodded her head furiously. Sam looked around the group and chuckled, "Our sweet wife decided it was okay to be sassy with her other Master today on the phone. I'm sure she thought she was perfectly safe since he was working on a rescue on the other side of the globe." He gave the chain a firm pull and smirked when Jen writhed on his lap. "What she didn't know was he and the others had successfully delivered that sweet little girl back to her family and were already on their way home. So our sweet doll here wasn't going to have time on her side for Sage to forget and forgive her transgression."

Carl Phillips was sitting next to Dex and as usual, his casual pose was a ruse. Anyone who had ever been on a mission with the man recognized the predator that lurked just under the surface. Carl had been one of the operatives who had gone to South America to rescue Jen and their bond of friendship had been solid ever since, despite her continuing comments about his wild driving. "Oh, sweet girl, you are in for it, aren't you? I just can't believe we went all the way to Bolivia to pull your pretty ass out of the fire only to have you put it on the line again."

His words and tsking sound seemed to pull Jen back from the edge and she leveled a look at him. "I have thanked Master Mario Petty for that rescue on several occasions and," Jen's sassy use of the nickname she'd given Carl—a combination of champion Formula1 racer Mario Andretti and NASCAR Hall of Famer, Richard Petty's names had been a deliberate distraction. Jen knew her husband well enough to know he'd paddle her ass for the comment and she was probably hoping it would pull her back from the edge—Dex doubted that was how it was going to play out and didn't even try to hold back his chuckle. Just as Sam lifted Jen from his lap, his brother stepped up behind him and lifted her right into his arms.

"Sweet cheeks, you are in a real pickle, you know that?" Dex watched as his friend's eyes softened as he took in his wife's startled expression and then squeal of delight when she realized who was holding her.

"Yes, I know and I'm trying to feel remorseful...really I am...but I'm just so fredding glad you are here that I just don't care. I don't care if you spank me…I just want you to touch me. God I missed you so much. Master Sam doesn't laugh at my jokes. He just looks at me like I'm a dork."

"Let's go, I need to be inside of you and then we're going to deal with your bratty behavior." Sage turned and walked purposefully toward the private rooms. His long legs ate up the distance quickly. Dex looked at Sam who was shaking his head.

"How am I ever going to train her properly when he does shit like that? Damn. And she's right about the jokes, half the time I have no clue what they are giggling about. But I'm glad Sage has a playmate because, honest to God, I've never understood his sense of humor."

Dex felt Meri stiffen and gave her a soft squeeze, "Sweetness, if you have something to say to Master Sam, you have permission to do so…respectfully." He wanted to laugh at her soft gasp of surprise, sometimes the woman was just too easy to read.

She recovered quickly and nodded before turning her attention to Sam. "Master Sam, I've talked to Jen several times and she has wonderful things to say about both you and your brother." She paused and seemed to be considering whether or not to continue before plunging ahead, "Well, I just thought it sounded as if you felt a bit left out because they share the same appreciation for silliness, and well, I didn't want you to be unhappy."

Sam McCall looked at Meri for long seconds before finally speaking. "Meri, I didn't mean to imply that at all. I'm confident in my relationship with Jen, my brother and I both bring very different things into her life. But…that being said, I want to thank you for being our friend and caring about how I felt. I rarely change my opinion about someone, but knowing you has reminded me why it's important to not make snap judgments." Dex rubbed his hand in soothing circles over Meri's shoulders when he felt her go rigid at Sam's words. He knew she hated the fact everyone's first impression of her had been so horribly negative. Sam's eyes softened and he shook his head, "I know that didn't come out at all right. What I was trying to say is that I'm glad I've gotten to know the real woman and I'm also grateful my wife has you for a friend. Friends who are willing to take the risk you just took are rare and I'm glad you are in her life." He stood and stretched, a sly smile curving his lips. "Now, I have a sub who needs a beating before my brother and I remind her what it feels like to have two cocks seeing to her pleasure."

"Even though I am flattered by the nickname, give your sweet subbie a couple of sound swats for me—I don't want her getting too cheeky." Carl Phillips' grin softened his expression, but Dex knew there was something bothering his friend and vowed to schedule a time for the two of them to spar, he'd always found a couple of rounds in the ring was good for finding out what was eating at someone. Carl turned his gaze back to the rest of the group as Sam strode away, "Are any of you up for watching the Wests christen the 'Woodshed'? I hear Tobi provided them with the perfect excuse this afternoon. Personally I just think she wanted to be first."

Dex had heard the club's newest feature was finally finished and fully functional, and he wasn't surprised the Wests would be christening the new area tonight. The Woodshed looked for all intents and purposes exactly like what the name implied—an old-fashioned wood shed used by many parents as a punishment location for their wayward offspring. The threat of being taken "behind the Woodshed" was often enough to set a progeny on the right path—hadn't worked that way for him, but his sisters had both only made the long journey to the backside of hell once to his knowledge.

When he and Ash had toured the new area with the other Masters in residence at the club last week, they'd been impressed with how realistic the entire setup was despite all the security monitoring and hidden BDSM elements. The woodpile itself was a fully functional spanking bench with sliding doors concealing a well-stocked supply cabinet complete with everything a Master might need to punish a naughty sub. There was also seating for an audience as well as several technological options allowing observers to participate.

All of the Masters now had apps on their phones that would allow them to "vote" on punishments, volunteer to help if a Master was of a mind to allow it, or provide input that could be sent to the group or any individual. Micah Drake had outdone himself on the tech end and every Master who had seen the venue had been impressed as hell. Dex would have loved nothing more than to make use of the Woodshed after the Wests scene, but they'd had to quickly change their plans after seeing Meri's colorful ass. Dex didn't see any reason they couldn't watch the scene though. He'd known several submissives who became as aroused from watching as they did from playing, and it would be interesting to see how Meri reacted. They'd noticed she was self-conscious about being exposed out in the open areas of the club and that was one of the boundaries he and Ash planned to push.

MERI FELT AS if her entire body was vibrating and they

hadn't even stepped out the club's back door yet. She'd heard Tobi, Gracie, and Regi mention the Woodshed but they'd all been banned from the area, so what little they knew was pure conjecture. Meri had never heard the expression "taken out behind the Woodshed," but the others had been more than happy to enlighten her on the American euphemism for paddling. Ash had taken one hand and Dex the other as they made their way down the walkway and Meri found herself trembling but she wasn't sure if it was from fear or anticipation. Ash paused and looked down at her, "Are you cold?"

Even though the outside air felt cool against her heated skin, Meri certainly didn't feel cold. *Nope, not cold at all. Holy hell, my blood feels like it may start to boil.* Meri's mind finally refocused on the moment and she realized she hadn't answered his question. "No, Sir, I'm not cold at all, even though I probably should be." His grin told her that he understood what she was implying.

"Good to know. So I'm assuming your trembling is from anticipation or apprehension. And I'm guessing that was what you were thinking through rather than answering my question." Even though it hadn't been a question, Meri still nodded her head in agreement. He smiled and she heard Dex's soft laughter behind her. "Let's go see what you think of the Wests' latest attempt to keep naughty subs in-line, although I suspect the area may not offer much in the line of punishment for some of you." With that he gave her ass a quick swat and turned back to the path.

Rounding the corner and taking in the venue, Meri was surprised to find it wasn't at all what she'd expected. It appeared to be remarkably rustic and so simple that she wondered why it had taken so long to construct. There were several rows of cushioned chairs spaced far enough apart to accommodate a kneeling submissive, and the raised stage area looked more like a simple movie set. Her confusion had probably shown in her expression because she heard both men chuckle. "Don't be fooled, this is a construction and technological wonder. The Prairie Winds staff truly has outdone themselves." Moving toward the front, Meri noticed that Tobi was already standing on the stage with her hands behind her back. The simple white cotton sheath was completely translucent with the lighting focused on her from all directions. Even though she was obviously supposed to be looking at the floor, Meri could see her eyes darting up occasionally. When she noticed Meri, her shoulders seemed to relax as if she had been looking for someone for moral support. Meri gasped as a feeling of pure panic moved through her. *Oh my God, don't they remember what Tobi's dad did to her? I have to help her.* She didn't even get to finish the thought when Ash spun her quickly so she was facing him. "Tell me."

Meri knew her breathing had kicked into high gear and she worried her heart might actually beat its way out of her chest, but she still knew exactly what he wanted. He'd sensed her anxiety and wanted to identify the trigger. Once she'd finally admitted her interest in the BDSM lifestyle, Meri had researched it tirelessly. One of the elements that attracted her was a Dom's commitment to caring for his submissive—both physically and emotionally. The concern was easy to see in his eyes and after a couple of deep breaths she finally answered, "I just sort of had a flashback to the stories Tobi's told me about her childhood…and well, I'm worried for her."

Ash nodded once letting her know he'd *heard* her concern, "Do you think Tobi's Masters will honor her use of the club's safe word?"

Meri was shocked by his question, it had never entered her mind that Kyle or Kent would ignore their wife's use of a safe word. Safe, sane, and consensual was the guiding tenant at Prairie Winds and *any* Dom not ending a scene immediately when the sub safe-worded out was banned for life. "Of course." At his raised brow she remembered where they were and quickly added "Sir" to the end.

"Do you think Kent and Kyle are the type of men to forget about the hell their beloved wife and submissive endured as a teenager?" Ash's tone was neutral, but she recognized the fact he was quickly painting her in to a corner with his questions.

"No, Sir."

"Hmmm, well then, the only other thing I can think of that might cause you this kind of distress is that you question whether or not Tobi will use her safe word if she needs to."

The truth was that she was concerned about that, but hadn't realized it when she'd panicked. So many of the people that surrounded Tobi at Prairie Winds saw her as this strong-willed woman with a core of steel. But Meri saw past that façade to the vulnerable woman beneath the brass and sass that was on the surface. Meri recognized that she and Tobi were actually very similar in a lot of ways, because they both measured themselves by how much they pleased the people they loved. Tobi would go to the ends of the earth to please her Masters and there was a very large part of Meri that understood that completely.

"Well...I hadn't really reasoned that all out when I got scared, but I think you are exactly right. I'm worried that she won't stop if she starts having a flashback. Mostly I am just worried for her." Meri felt a tear trail slowly down her cheek but she didn't move to wipe it away, she continued to hold Ash's gaze as he studied her closely.

He finally took a deep breath and sat down. Once he had her kneeling between his thighs, he cupped her face in his large hands. Using his thumbs to brush away her tears, he smiled, "You are so fucking beautiful—inside and out, pet. I want you to stop and think about how much Kent and Kyle West love Tobi. They don't see her as their sub, she is their heart. I know them like I know myself and Dex, and I can assure you their happiness is linked so closely with hers that none of them knows where one starts and the other ends. Both of them are truly Masters of all the dynamics of Dominance and submission, they know exactly what their woman needs and they are going to give it to her because she wants it so badly."

Meri was lost in his words and kept rolling them around in her mind in the way that she always did when she was considering every possible angle of a problem or question. Ash didn't say anything for several minutes, but finally leaned forward and kissed her lightly on the tip of her nose. "Make me a promise as you watch this scene—I want you to ignore Tobi as much as you can. Focus your attention on her Masters. Watch them closely and you will see they are entirely centered on the woman they both love beyond measure. She won't take a breath that they don't see. At every juncture of the scene, they'll be able to tell you her heart and respiration rate as well as how it has changed over the course of the scene. They'll know within a millisecond when she is to the point of no return and they'll pull her back as many times as they think she can stand. When one of them is administering a punishment, the other will be watching...assessing...monitoring...loving."

Dex used his fingers under her chin to bring her attention to him and spoke quietly, "Watch them and see if you don't recognize some of those behaviors, sweetness."

Just as she was about to ask him what he meant, the lights dimmed and Ash leaned down and adjusted the large pillow she was kneeling on so she was facing the front. "Knees further apart, pet. Remember, that pussy belongs to us and we'll damned well show it off if it pleases us." He slipped a fur-lined leather cuff on one wrist and Dex did the same on her other side. Once they'd positioned her arms behind her back, she heard the distinctive snick of metal and realized they'd hooked her wrists together so that her back was a graceful arch that thrust her breasts forward. She was grateful they had allowed her to wear one of their dress shirts even though she was bare beneath the thin linen. She'd gotten several swats for simply planning to wear panties earlier in the day and they had explained in great detail how much worse it would have been had she actually put on the offensive garments. *Offensive garments? Seriously? Who talks like that? When she'd made the mistake of uttering that question out loud, they had each given her another swat for being cheeky. Personally she thought cheeky was archaic as well, but her burning ass reminded her of the wisdom of keeping that to herself.*

Chapter Fourteen

ASH WATCHED MERI with the same intensity she studied the Wests. He was certain she would be able to recall every nuance of the entire scene. One of the many things they'd learned about her in the past few days was that she had a memory that was as close to a camera as anything he could imagine. She'd given them a scientific explanation that had been full of psychobabble and bullshit, but the bottom line was, if the woman saw it, heard it, or read it— she knew it—frontward, backward, and inside out. They'd playfully tested her one night by flipping through a movie scene involving a car chase that he'd watched a dozen times before he'd noticed all the details she'd recited in such a blasé manner he'd wondered for a moment if she'd seen the movie before. She'd simply laughed and waved them off. "The doctors have done these tests with me so many times. I used to try to view them as a game, because outside of that, it was damned annoying."

Anyone who had listened to Kent recount for the audience all of Tobi's transgressions had known immediately the little imp was topping from the bottom. After the lengthy list, Kent had turned to her and simply said, "Forgiven." Tobi's expression had been priceless. Hell, you would have thought someone had just kicked her new puppy. Ash had to cover his laugher with a cough and he heard several other Masters do the same. After several long seconds, Kent had crossed his arms and stared at his disappointed sub with a look of frustration that he rarely used on her. Kyle mirrored his stance and look, but Kent was the one who held her gaze captive with his own. "What we *do* plan to deal with however, is the fact you have been topping from the bottom in ways that neither of us have ever even seen in books or training films. Hell, we should probably write a fucking book because you, sweetness, are in a class all your own."

Kyle stepped forward and turned her face toward his own, "Kitten, the real problem here is that you needed us and rather than asking for what you needed, you acted out. And at the core of *that* is a lack of trust—and in the end it doesn't matter whether it's us or yourself that you are questioning, because as your Masters, the buck always stops here." He emphasized his point by pointing to himself and then to Kent.

Ash saw the tears rolling down Meri's cheeks but knew they were simply an indication of how connected she felt to the scene. He reached forward and placed his hand on the top of her shoulder and squeezed gently. They continued to watch as Tobi was secured between two large wooden posts that rose from their hiding places beneath the floor. He smiled when he heard the collective gasp of the subs in the room as the Wests started showcasing some of the Woodshed's unique features. Once Tobi was secured at both ankles and wrists, Kent wrapped a thick belt around her tiny waist and locked it tightly between the posts as well before tilting the entire apparatus forward approximately twenty degrees.

Ash knew the angle was enough to give Tobi the illusion of falling but more importantly, it would help Kyle pull the lashes he planned to give her. Tobi was going to feel a fast line of fire race over her skin, but it would be gone within a few seconds. What she was going to truly experience was the uncertainty of what they were going to do and the anticipation of pain would be tied directly to the sound of the single tail as it split the air with a deafening crack. Kent was standing directly in front of Tobi, he made sure she acknowledged and understood her safe word, and also made her explain to him when she was supposed to use it. Once both Doms were satisfied that she was ready, the first lash fell and a thin red line appeared before quickly fading. Tobi's gasp had probably been more from the startling sound than the sting, but Kent held up his palm holding back the next lash while he spoke softly to her. They had both turned off their lapel mikes, but Ash knew Kent was checking her emotional state. This scene had been planned down to the gnat's ass and both Wests had picked the brains of their core group of Masters until they'd all groaned when it was even mentioned.

This was the first major scene they'd had at the club since Tobi had given birth to the twins and Kent and Kyle were both nervous as hell about pushing her too far. Oddly enough they'd expressed the same concern Meri had—that Tobi would be so caught up in her desire to please them she wouldn't safe word out if she truly needed to. It had been Peter Weston who had come up with this plan, and Ash noticed him standing just off stage. It was only at his nod that the scene resumed. With each lash Tobi's response was more moan than gasp and the lines seemed to linger longer as well, so he knew Kyle was slowly intensifying the experience for her. Before the last lash fell, Kent flicked on his lapel mike before sliding his fingers through her soaking folds. And then at the precise moment the lash landed, his command, "Come for us, love," boomed over the speakers.

Tobi's scream filled the open area at the same time Ash heard the clatter of the single-tail's handle on the stage floor. Both men were inside her within seconds and even from his place several feet away, Tobi's second climax was easy to see. Kent had caught the second scream in his kiss but the waves of release could be seen in the rippling through her muscles. When Ash leaned down so his face was beside Meri's, he could see fresh tears streaming down her face. "Pet?"

"That was amazing. And I wouldn't have ever seen it if you hadn't told me to watch her Masters." She still hadn't taken her eyes off the stage and he was glad she was watching how tenderly they cared for Tobi now that they had regained their footing after what appeared to have been soul-shattering releases. There had been a lot of pressure on both men tonight and Ash was glad it had gone well.

Ash could smell her arousal and smiled when Dex slid his fingers through her pussy lips and the wet sounds were easily heard above the buzz of conversation around them. *Seems our pretty subbie enjoyed watching as much as we'd hoped she would—perfect.*

Dex had listened as Ash led Meri through a carefully planned dance of words during their earlier conversation, he couldn't hold back his smile when she realized how he was leading her, but to her credit she had continued to follow. It was a small sign of her growing trust in them, but he was thankful he'd had the chance to witness it. When a submissive entrusted you with her body it was heady stuff to be sure, but knowing they'd put their soul in your care was the dream of every sexual Dominant Dex knew. Physical surrender was easy to coax from a woman, hell, teenage boys did it all the time. But being able to connect to a sub's soul was the most powerful aphrodisiac known to man in Dex's opinion.

Watching Meri as she followed Ash's command to focus her attention on Tobi's Masters had been fascinating. The emotions played out over her beautiful face in Technicolor and Dex had been grateful for the front row seat. He was willing to wager that for the first time she'd seen the intensity a good Dom brought to each scene. Being an effective sexual Dominant was never as simple as barking out orders, even though users and abusers regularly tried to play it that way. Those men and women rarely even made it through the Prairie Winds' stringent screening process. Micah and Jax's vetting process caught most wanna-bes, but any who managed to slip through that net were snagged during the personal interview with Kyle and Kent.

Hell, he and Ash had worked with all four men for years, but had still been required to go through each stage of the process before they'd been allowed to play at the club. The entire process had been a royal pain in the ass, but some of their questions had been thought provoking enough to make him consider closely exactly what it was he was looking for in a submissive. In the end, both he and Ash had been forced to consider carefully about where they were heading in life—something his family had been after him to think about for a very long time.

The lengthy interview had forced him to think back on his sister, Lizzy's, words Christmas morning a few years earlier when she'd essentially told him he'd become another person, it had annoyed him at first. But it had also led him to recount the night several months later when he'd been lying under the vast starlit sky on a mountaintop in bum-fuck-classified-nowhere when he had been struck with the realization she'd been absolutely right. He'd often wondered how it was that a tiny bit of a thing with four wild kids had been the one to approach a glowering Navy SEAL and call a spade a spade. *Fuck, dealing with those four yard apes of hers probably takes nerves of steel—I was probably a walk in the damned park.*

Reaching down and sliding his fingers through her silken pussy lips made Meri moan and a fresh rush of cream coat his fingers. Dex knew full well he could fuck her with his fingers and bring her to climax in under a minute, but they had different plans for the gorgeous woman kneeling between them. Biting down on the shell of her ear, he let his words whisper over her skin, "Not yet, sweetheart. You hold that orgasm back or you'll not get another one in a good, long while. We have plans for you, but I want you to know we are very pleased with how you responded to watching the scene. I can practically hear the wheels of that brilliant mind of yours spinning."

Glancing up, he noted Ash's quick nod and pulled his fingers out of her pulsing sheath just as Ash slid the small remote controlled egg deep inside. Dex wanted to laugh because he didn't even think she realized what had happened. Meri had been working so hard to fight off her release, her entire focus was on that task and she'd missed a very important detail. They both pulled their hands from her and sucked her juices from their fingers bring her to her feet as they stood.

"Come along, pet, we have business to take care of before we see to your pleasure." Her eyes were still glazed over with arousal—a look that was fast becoming his personal favorite, as they led her to the stage. They had pre-arranged with the Masters who planned to be in attendance to turn their subs away from the stage or blindfold them during their scene. They'd known the bruising on her ass and legs would be misinterpreted by some and likely frighten others who didn't know about Meri's particular kink. A few had chosen to leave because they were spending the evening with newbie subs. Those Masters hadn't known exactly how the novices would react to being blindfolded and they hadn't trusted the little darlings to keep from peeking either.

Dex turned Meri so her back was to the audience as he explained how unhappy he and Ash had been when they'd seen what their lovely submissive had chosen to conceal from them. His dramatized version brought smiles to the Masters' faces. No one had to worry about monitoring their reactions since none of the submissives present could see them. Stepping back, he watched as Ash began unbuttoning the shirt she was wearing. "Sir?"

"Be still, pet." Ash's words might have been commanding but his tone was soft and he was relieved to see her shoulders relax fractionally. Her silent nod followed and Dex watched as Ash pushed the shirt slowly over her shoulders and it slid in a silent whisper over her luscious curves until it puddled at her feet. Even though the other Masters had been briefed in advance, their wide-eyed reaction was genuine. Many cursed out loud, and frowns of concern replaced their earlier smiles. Ash's fingers held her chin tipped up so she was focused on his face and Dex saw her biting her lip, something he'd noticed she did when she felt particularly vulnerable.

"As you can see, we're caught in something of a dilemma here. Further impact punishment is not an option for a couple of reasons. First of all she'd like it far too much." When the chuckles died down as he went on, "But most importantly, her health and well-being are not only our privilege—they are our responsibility as well. What our sub fails to understand is that scenes are a very small piece of the picture." Just as he stepped to the side, Dex heard the distinctive sound of a camera shutter. It sounded as if it had come from the small curtained off area to his left, but he hadn't been sure until he saw the curtain sway ever so slightly. It didn't take long for him to realize he hadn't been the only one to hear it.

Peter tossed him one of the soft subbie blankets used for aftercare as he sprinted past them. Dex quickly wrapped Meri in the blanket and sat her with the other subs that were now huddled together in front of the stage. Their Masters had ordered them to stay together before taking off in various directions. After seeing the terrified expression on Meri's face, Dex decided against joining his teammates. He knew her fear wasn't for her physical safety—after all, cameras were rarely deadly in his experience, but the images they captured certainly held catastrophic potential.

Meri had already confided that John Stevens' threats to expose her lifestyle choices was what she feared the most. She'd said on several occasions she didn't believe the man would harm her physically. Hell, he wouldn't need to—all he had to do was see to it compromising pictures of Meri were *leaked* to the media. Even if they were suppressed, the rumors and innuendo alone would devastate her reputation. He'd reap all the *shattered boyfriend* points with the public and the future Meri had always envisioned for herself would be left in shreds.

During his last few missions, Dex had sworn the earbud communication devices they wore had been designed by Satan himself. Newbie team members tended to chatter endlessly when they were nervous and the more seasoned members of a squad often wanted to send the small bits of electronics sailing off the nearest tall structure. Tonight was the first time he realized how much he'd depended upon the ability to speak with his fellow soldiers. This might not hold the same deadly potential they were accustomed to facing, but it was damned well as important. Glancing around the small group of subs sitting together speaking quietly among themselves, Dex realized that each of them had her own reasons for worrying about public exposure. Several were prominent businesswomen, one was a prosecutor, and he'd just recently learned the eldest in the group was a federal judge. *Oh yeah, a prosecutor and a judge? Score a big one for the good guys if they could catch whoever had taken that shot.*

Chapter Fifteen

KYLE WEST HAD just laid his sweet, sleeping wife on the bed when he saw his phone flashing on the dresser across the room. He'd left very specific instruction with his staff that neither he nor Kent wanted to be disturbed unless it was an absolute do-or-die emergency, so he quickly covered Tobi before grabbing the phone and heading out of the room. By the time he'd finished listening to Jax's message, he was enraged. Knowing someone had willfully violated one of the club's cardinal rules by bringing in an electronic device that had not been pre-approved infuriated him, but the realization that everyone in attendance tonight had potentially been compromised terrified him.

Privacy guarantees were at the core of every kink club's survival, so securing the camera and the culprit were his chief concerns. Hearing the shower turn off, he knew Kent would notice his phone's message light momentarily. Staring out the large windows overlooking the acreage between the club and the river, Kyle sighed as he noticed a small watercraft racing down the opposite shore toward Austin. There was a larger craft following but he already knew without a miracle they weren't going to resolve this tonight. When he heard a soft noise by the door, Kyle turned expecting to see his brother but was surprised to see Tobi standing there—the soft light from tonight's full moon highlighting every lush curve of her naked beauty.

For a few seconds he was completely speechless—simply lost in his gratitude for the heaven sent flash of lightning that had kept him from hitting her that night on the highway.

"I woke up alone. And since that doesn't happen often I was worried. Is everything alright? You look worried." Her sweet concern touched his heart and he simply held out his hand to her, pleased beyond measure that she immediately moved into his arms.

"No, kitten, I'm afraid things are definitely not alright. There has been a major security breach and I'm afraid Kent and I are both going to be heading downstairs. I don't have any idea how long we'll be, but I don't want you to wait up for us. Mom and the dads are bringing the kids back in the morning so you need to get some sleep." Scooping her up into his arms he walked reluctantly back to the bedroom. Damn he hated leaving her alone after what they'd shared tonight. It had been their first public scene in over a year and it couldn't have been any more perfect. The lashes had burned an even deeper connection between the three of them despite the fact he'd pulled them to the point they'd been little more than noise. She'd had spankings that caused her more pain, but pain hadn't been anything close to what they'd been trying to achieve. The entire scene had been a mind game intended to remind the love of their life they intended to meet each and every one of her needs— she only had to ask. Sure there would be things they would deny her...but she needed to know those would be explained and most often involve hers or their children's safety.

Leaning forward to kiss her goodbye Kyle had to push back his desire to simply shed the well-worn jeans he was wearing and sink into her sweet body. Losing himself inside her heat sounded like a perfect way to avoid the unpleasantness that awaited him downstairs.

JAX WASN'T SURE he ever remembered being as angry as he had been when the sound of a camera shutter registered in his mind during Dex and Ash's scene with Meri. The split second it had taken him to move Gracie to safety had almost kept him from seeing the perp disappear into the thick shrubs along the back of the Woodshed. Once he'd begun crawling under the foliage, he'd immediately realized he was pursuing a woman because whoever she was—she was easily sliding under the prickly branches. There was a grace and fluidity to her movements that seemed familiar, but he wasn't going to take time to figure it out now. Once he was back on his feet, he pushed in the ear bud that he always kept in his pocket anytime he was on the club's property whether or not he was working. It had been a precautionary habit before they'd had adequate staff, and he was grateful now it was one he hadn't broken.

Whoever he was chasing was damned fast on their feet and knew exactly where they were going, too. He'd alerted the others that they were heading for the dock. Jax watched men race toward the small wooden boat dock from all directions and was shocked to see the perp pause long enough to stash something in a small backpack. She was trying to slide the pack's straps over her shoulders when Peter reached her. His grip locked on the nylon bag and before he could get a hand on the woman she slipped free of the bag's unbuckled straps before diving smoothly into the dark water.

Three former Navy SEALs hit the surface right behind

her but the inky black river seemed to have swallowed her whole. Ash, Carl, and Peter all surfaced at the same time, their mutters of frustration quickly turned to full-blown cursing when they heard a Jet Ski start up a few yards away. Jax was already headed to the Wests' larger boat and wasn't far behind, but the smaller craft's maneuverability meant the intruder easily evaded capture. By the time Jax returned to the dock there was a small crowd waiting for him, including Kyle and Kent West.

"Peter, did you get your hands on her?" Jax knew if Peter had managed to touch her there was a distinct possibility he'd be able to ID her later.

"No, but I caught her energy signature so if I get near her again I'll know it. I'm assuming you knew it was a woman because of the way she moved?" When Jax nodded, Peter smiled, "Dance background, mark my word. The woman loves to dance and probably does it anytime there's music playing."

"And you got the bag, right?"

Kyle held up the bag, "I have it now, let's get up to the office and see what we've got." Turning to the men who were still standing in their wet clothing, "Shower, change, then meet us in the office. We'll stop by the Woodshed and gather the subs Dex has been watching over." Everyone dispersed and Jax quickly finished securing the boat before making his way back up the gentle slope. In all the years he and Kyle West had served together in the Special Forces, Jax wasn't sure he'd ever seen the man this angry. Rubbing his hand over his face, Jax wondered if Meri had been the only target and how on earth he was going to explain this to Chandler Lanham. Meri's dad had paid him a small fortune to update the security system at their home and then she is compromised at the kink club where he works as the chief of security. Yeah, that's going to go over like a lead balloon. *Fuck me...I really have to get some damned sleep.*

KYLE AND KENT West's office was enormous but it suddenly seemed entirely too small. Tobi had invited the submissives to the rooftop garden for an impromptu margarita party since the twins were spending the night with the elder Wests, and their Masters had been grateful for her quick thinking. Jen had been given the option of staying downstairs since she was a member of the team, but Dex had a sneaking suspicion she was acting more as an informant for her friends than she was in an official capacity. It didn't really matter, none of them would hide this information from their subs anyway—you can't demand transparency on their part if you aren't willing to do the same.

Everyone had been relieved when the bag had yielded nothing but a snorkel and a small waterproof camera. The camera was fairly sophisticated, but didn't have any wireless potential so there wasn't any chance of the photos being shared. It hadn't taken Micah Drake long to access the small electronic camera and begin a slide show on the wall above the fireplace. Dex and Ash had watched in stunned silence as picture after picture of the two of them flashed on the makeshift screen. *What the fuck?* All were shots taken without their knowledge and most were taken at Prairie Winds.

They'd sat through so many shots that Micah had finally scanned forward to see what else was on the small disc. "Someone has a major hard-on for you two. Any ideas?" Kyle's voice was serious, but lacked any of the anger they'd all felt earlier. Once he'd discovered they had recovered the only photos taken, he'd calmed down and seemed to be thinking with a clearer head. When Ash and Dex both stared at him, Kyle finally chuckled, "Christ, guys, what's with the deer in the headlights looks. It wasn't that hard of a question."

Before either he or Ash could respond, pictures of Meri started appearing on the wall. There were only a few shots before Micah switched it back to his laptop. "I don't think I want to project the rest of these. But you guys need to come and look at this." They stood and moved to the desk, Dex felt a rolling wave of rage boil up inside of him that literally had him seeing red. The small camera had obviously been mounted on some kind of scope and the pictures taken through the large windows lining the back of the Lanham mansion clearly showed someone had been watching the night they'd punished Meri over the table. Dex heard Ash's growl as the pictures moved over the small screen highlighting each and every strike. The intensity of Ash's expression made him look like a monster and Dex knew his friend was seeing exactly what he saw.

Chapter Sixteen

ASH LEANED AGAINST the railing surrounding the small deck at the back of the office and looked out over the sparkling water of the West's private pool. The fading moonlight glittered along the surface like small diamonds and, had his stomach not been threatening to revolt, he might have actually found the scene peaceful. He wasn't sure how long he'd been standing outside, only that he hadn't been able to stay in the office another minute. The walls had been closing in quickly and for the first time he could remember, he'd actually run from a problem.

Two things had become crystal clear while he'd been looking at the pictures. First of all, he and Dex had to reevaluate the way they handled Meri, because there was no way he'd ever be able to punish her that harshly again. After seeing the bruising and then the photographic evidence of himself during the scene, he just couldn't imagine ever participating in another scene like that one. He'd always considered himself a borderline sadist, but he'd gotten no pleasure from looking at those pictures. *Where the fuck was my mind?*

His entire adult life, Ash had known exactly who he was—or at least he'd always believed he had, until tonight. Standing behind Kyle's desk, looking at picture after picture of himself, the only thing he'd known for certain was that he was never going to be that submerged in naïveté again.

How a former Special Forces operative who'd been a sexual Dominant his entire adult life could suddenly have such a crises of consciousness was a mystery to him, but it had still happened. Looking out over the sparkling water, he couldn't hold back his sigh.

"You okay?" Dex's voice sounded from right next to him and it was a testament to his distraction that he hadn't heard his friend approach.

"Fuck if I know. I looked at myself in those pictures and some of them made me...Jesus, I don't even know what. Seeing the look on my face as I punished Meri almost made me sick. That wasn't about mutual pleasure, that was anger. As a Dom I know better than that, hell, as a *man* I know better. For a split second I saw my brother's face over mine and my sweet sister-in-law's over Meri's and I wanted to kill him."

Turning to Dex, he asked, "What if that were one of your sisters? What would you think if you saw one of your brothers-in-law punishing Sarah or Lizzy like that? Hell, you saw the look on her face. That wasn't sexual pleasure, that was sheer strength of character enduring something brutally painful because she was seeking the approval of the person causing her pain. Can you stand there and tell me that you didn't see what I saw?"

Dex didn't respond for so long Ash was beginning to think he wasn't going to bother. Truth be told, his friend's blank expression was a response in itself. Dex knew him better than anyone else in the world. They often knew what the other one was thinking even before they spoke, but right now Ash had no idea where Dex's head was because he was too bogged down in the quagmire of his own emotions.

The silence finally proved to be too much and Ash said,

"Look, man, forget I said anything. This is my problem and I'll deal with it."

Dex's gaze centered on him immediately, "Fuck you, Ash. You think you were the only one sickened by those pictures? Hell, I have always known I wasn't a sadist, shit I'm nothing close to that, but I was right there with you that night, so don't even start this bullshit with me." Ash was stunned at the ferocity of his friend's response. Dex was usually the cool head that prevailed when Ash often reacted emotionally, so hearing his friend's frustration was sobering. "Listen, the only thing I am sure about at this point is everything in me is shouting that Meri is the miracle we've been looking for." Dex took a deep breath and pushed his fingers through his hair as he clearly waged an inner battle to remain calm. "Realizing someone is targeting her because of us cut me off at the fucking knees, man. If anything happens to her...*fuck!*" Several seconds later he leveled a look at Ash, "All I'm saying is that our first priority is to see to her safety. After all this is done, then we'll be able to figure out the rest. For now, the only thing that matters is fixing this disaster. We'll figure the rest of it out later. Let's get back inside and find out what the plan is. Kyle was in full mission mode when I left so we need to be brought up to speed."

Making their way back inside, Ash heard Kent's voice, "Call every member that was here tonight and explain to them what we're planning. Make sure they fully understand so they are particularly careful in their conversations with any members who weren't here tonight. Whoever is responsible for these photos is obviously a member or has access and we don't want to alert her. We also don't know for sure if she's working alone, if we had more time we could piece together which nights these were taken and crosscheck the attendance lists, but we don't have that luxury. And everyone—and I do mean everyone, people, walks past Peter tomorrow night."

AFTER SLEEPING FAR less than she'd have liked, Meri found herself back at the club helping with phone calls to the members who had been in attendance the night before. Most were relieved to hear the Wests had a *plan* even though the details weren't being shared. When she'd inquired about Regi, Dex had explained the recent email she'd received from her father. "None of us really believed she had actually seen him on that boat because we'd watched the wreckage tumble into the abyss—I would have sworn no one could have survived that." Meri saw him shake his head as if he was still trying to wrap his mind around the truth.

"Is it possible it's not really him?"

"Absolutely. And that is why her men are accompanying her to the meeting. They actually wanted to meet with him alone first, but Regi was not exactly what you would call *on board* with that plan, as you can well imagine. They are meeting for an early dinner this evening at a small place along the river. Kyle called in some favors and a couple of guys we know from the teams who are on leave will be standing by just in case things go from sugar to shit."

She knew she was just staring at him dumbfounded, but the whole story was just so insane she could barely take it all in. Meri was quickly learning she'd led an incredibly sheltered life, that there were things happening all around her that she'd never imagined possible…and the realization had been humbling.

MERI KNEW ASH and Peter's description of the woman's height and weight was going to help narrow down the suspects, but she couldn't help asking one more time if they had contacted Trac Hughes. Tobi had ordered take-out for everyone and they were all relaxing in the club's large main lounge when Meri posed the question. Kyle West looked up and nodded, "We did, and he's coming by sometime after eight this evening. It seems the good senator has a fundraising dinner and after the Rangers questioned him about the break-in at your place, he's been in full victim mode. Somehow the self-centered pissant has managed to flip everything around to where the break-in was the perp's way of getting to him." Meri could only stare at Kyle, she was speechless but not really all that shocked John had managed to mind-fuck everyone with the information, turning it into something that would benefit himself. The man was a first class media manipula-tor, hell, he could have made Judas look like a victim.

Evidently she'd been lost in thought long enough to draw attention because Dex's hand gently squeezing her knee brought her back to the moment, his eyes reflecting his concern, "You okay?"

"Yes, I'm sorry. I just have trouble understanding how easily he can switch things up to put himself at the center of every storm. It's remarkable really."

"Yeah, remarkable—too bad Mr. Remarkable doesn't use his super powers for good." Tobi's voice dripped sarcasm and made Meri giggle, which was probably exactly what her friend had been going for. "I met Mr. Ego Extraordinaire one day when Meri and I had lunch together. He stopped by our table with some of his *supporters*. And by the way, every time he used that word I got a mental picture of a jock strap—totally disgusting. Anyway, I agree with Meri, he isn't *enough* to be behind all this. Besides, I'll bet his idea of kinky sex is doing it on the living room sofa. Hell, he even walks like he has a stick up his ass, so I can't see him wanting to see pics of his ex-girlfriend enjoying what he couldn't give her. I mean, I'm not a guy, so maybe I'm off base here, but I don't think so."

Every Dom in the room was gawking at Tobi as if she'd just spoken in tongues, and Meri couldn't hold back the giggle that bubbled up inside her. *God I love her, she brings the most amazing realism into my life. I hope her colorful personality is contagious.* The giggle was part nervous reaction and part sheer joy but more than anything it was a release valve that seemed to drain away the tension she'd been bottling up. The ability to defuse stressful situations was one of Tobi West's most amazing gifts if you asked Meri…and she'd seen the tiny blonde do it time and again, often at the expense of her backside. More than once Meri had looked on as Tobi deliberately acted out just to distract attention from someone she was trying to help or protect. Her husbands understood her motives, but punished her anyway, probably because she enjoyed it so much.

Tobi finally sensed the silence and looked up from her plate with such a beguilingly confused look that Meri nearly rolled her eyes. "What? Just because I speak the unvarnished truth doesn't mean you all have to look at me like I'm speaking Pekinese or something."

"That's it. Kent, we have to start rationing her access to Mom." Kyle then turned toward his wife's faux innocent expression. "Don't even try that look with me, kitten, I'm wise to your ways. And if Kent's mother teaches this nonsense to Tobi, I'll be positively pissed."

"Christ, now you've done it. How many times have I told you not to do that? Damn it, it's like summoning a dem-angel, you speak their name and they magically appear."

"Good save...almost, my precious son." Lily West had indeed seemed to materialize out of thin air and her patronizing tone didn't fool anyone. "Now, Kyle dear, as to me teaching the lovely ladies in your life how to deal with your bossy self, it's my duty and privilege." When Kyle rolled his eyes, his mom reached forward and swatted him upside the head and the entire room erupted into uproarious laughter. Meri might not have heard Lilly's next words if she hadn't been sitting so close, "Don't mess with the mommy monster when she hasn't had all her beauty sleep, my darling son. You really should know better." *Okay, I stand corrected, I hope Lilly and Tobi are both contagious.*

Chapter Seventeen

REGI WAS TREMBLING despite the waning sunshine warming her shoulders as she and her fiancés walked hand in hand down the wide sidewalk curving along the river's edge. The closer they got to the small café were her father planned to meet them, the more apprehensive she became. Brian Bennett paused and turned Regi so she faced him, "Sweetness, are you sure you're ready for this? We can go in and check it out first." Regi felt her eyes fill with tears, but she was resolute in her determination to keep them from falling. She'd been giving herself mental pep talks for her entire adult life and she was to see this meeting through, come hell or high water.

Before she could answer, Regi felt Kirk press himself against her back and then lean down to kiss the tender spot behind her ear that always made her knees weak. "*Anoshi*, I am worried about you. We don't want anything or anyone upsetting you." Regi loved his Navajo nickname for her, hearing him use the Native American endearment for "my love" touched a part of her heart no one else had ever reached. The connection she felt to each of them was so deep she continually wondered why she'd fought the attraction for so long.

"I'll be okay, and this is something I have to do. No one else can answer the questions I have, and the only way to do it is to just push past my fear." Both men were now standing in front of her and nodded in perfect unison. She couldn't help but smile because it was as if they'd practiced the move, their synchronized movements often reminded her of the years they'd spent together. Regi hoped that someday she'd be able to mirror them as well as they did one another, and that she'd learn to anticipate their needs with the same amazing accuracy they seemed to have knowing hers.

Stepping in to the small eatery, Regi's gaze locked on her dad instantly. The minute their eyes met she saw him take a deep breath and then stand. She didn't wait for the hostess to seat them, instead she made her way to him, weaving between the tables until she stood in front of him and let her eyes take in everything. The last time she'd seen him this close he'd been wearing scuba gear and the only thing she'd recognized were his eyes. But now, standing face to face, the memories washed over her in a tidal wave of emotion she hadn't been expecting and wasn't convinced she welcomed. Kirk wrapped his arm around her waist and she felt herself relax into his embrace.

Brian took care of the introductions and once they were seated and had placed their drink orders, Regi couldn't hold back any longer. She knew her one word question, "Why?" was dripping with frustration and impatience, but she really didn't care. After all, how can anyone call her impatient when her life had been tossed end-over-end for an entire decade?

She watched him draw in a deep breath before speaking, "Greed, arrogance, selfishness, youthful ignorance, ego...pick one, hell, they all apply." Sighing deeply, he leaned forward clasping his hands in front of him on top of the small table. "I wanted to prove to the family that I had what it took to succeed without them. Their interference had always rankled me, it knew no bounds and to be honest, I had always failed miserably when conformity was required. I wanted the respect of my colleagues and business associates, but I wanted it based on what I'd done myself, not who I was related to. And I wanted my mother to see me as an adult who could make it on his own."

Once again Regi saw a deep sadness and a pain so raw reflected in his eyes it tugged at her heartstrings despite her attempts to stay distant. When she didn't respond, merely waiting for him to continue, she would have sworn she saw a small glimmer of hope, before he masked it. "Well, as you know, in the end I had to run back to the family with my tail between my legs. The net was being pulled in all around me very quickly…" Regi wondered why he'd gone to the trouble to stage his and her mother's deaths but he'd left her swinging in the breeze. "The agency wanted me to *come in* but I'd seen their re-identification and re-location services and knew none of us would ever be safe."

Kirk looked at her dad and asked, "Who was after you? And why would you be willing to leave your daughter behind?" To anyone near them Kirk's voice had probably sounded indifferent and only mildly interested, but Regi had heard the underlying threat in his tone.

"Who wasn't? Hell, my own family was even trying to reel me in, that's why they were able to stage everything so quickly. And leaving Regi behind was the only way to ensure her safety. She was safe if everyone believed her mother and I were dead. To those who wanted the information I'd gained, her only value was as leverage and they wouldn't have hesitated to use her to gain my compliance." They must not have seemed convinced because he looked between them and then back at his folded hands,

"You have to remember the high tech world you know today was just starting a decade ago. Information wasn't as easy to obtain as it is now and those who had it were extremely valuable for a short period of time. I'd planned to return for you in just a few months—Charlie was the answer to a prayer because we knew each other but weren't close enough for anyone to really suspect him, and he happened to be in Belize at the time. Honestly I couldn't believe my luck when I heard he was so close. And then it was like the angels had heard my plea when he was assigned to you."

"Who were the people under those sheets? Who died so you could hide? Do you know how many nights I woke up screaming because I'd had to step in your blood?" Regi felt her anger begin to boil to the surface and felt herself quaking from the barely contained rage. Seeing the first tear roll down his cheek, she sat back and crossed her arms over her chest, "Don't. You haven't earned the right to cry for me. Tell me the rest." She knew he hadn't expected her strength and there was a certain satisfaction in that fact. Regi understood that forgiving him was going to be about letting go and not allowing the memories to hurt her any longer, but she was determined to know everything first.

Her father sat silently across from her for so long Regi wasn't sure he was going to begin again. He stared endlessly with unseeing eyes at something over her left shoulder until she was actually tempted to turn around to see what held his gaze. A large part of her knew what he was looking at but not seeing, but she couldn't hold back her frustrated exhale. Her dad's focus returned to her and this time the depth of his despair stole her breath.

"I had promised myself and my beloved Nalia that I'd return for you quickly, but then when she died...the bottom fell out of my world." Regi could see him struggling to pull strength from within himself and she wondered if he would succeed when he looked at her with abject sincerity and said, "If you don't believe anything else I've told you, please know that I loved your mother with everything in me. Losing her tore my soul in two and left me little more than a shell of myself. I spent years doing exactly what you just witnessed—staring at nothing in particular. I floated in a fog of emptiness, caring little if I lived or died."

Regi listened as her dad explained the details of her life from his perspective and realized the love she'd thought he had for her was so tied to her mother, for all intents and purposes, she'd nearly lost him yet again when her mother died. Hearing all the details and knowing how easily she'd been fooled was humiliating. When she said as much all three men reminded her that she'd been far too young to understand everything that had been happening around her. "Listen, there was no way you could have known. I wasn't even completely honest with your mom, even though it turned out that she knew far more than I was aware of—that was why she'd begun coding things."

"Why was the map so important? I understand the gold bars and artifacts were valuable, but..."

"So perceptive and wise, just like your mother. God, she would have been so proud of the woman you've become. You're right, there was a lot of value that was easy to see, but what you didn't see was the secondary treasure that was buried nearby. I recovered that after you and the others left. It was actually fairly easy because you all thought I'd died." She knew her confusion showed and his small smile let her know he'd noted her questioning look. "Sometimes, very valuable things are very small, little red bird." Regi felt the air rush from her lungs at his use of the pet name he'd given her when she'd been a small child. Kirk's hand gripped her knee, his touch soothing because his firm hold reminded her of their connection. Brian had taken one of her hands to hold between his own, drawing slow circles over her palm. Her father's eyes flitted between the men as if taking in their ministrations before he continued, "Information, even when it is dated, that proves connections between people is valuable. At times the value is to those who seek the proof, but more often the value is to those who prefer to hide the truth." His words might have been cryptic, but the message was clear, he had the goods on someone…probably several people, and intended to market it.

"I've given away most of what I recovered. I don't have any money. Why did you contact me?" Regi hadn't intended to even ask and she certainly hadn't intended to just blurt the question out, but there it was.

For long seconds he appeared too stunned to answer, but slowly a hesitant smile moved over his face. "I know what you've done with the money and I'm humbled by the person you have become. Truthfully, I have more money than I could spend in several lifetimes so that isn't ever going to be an issue between us." His pause was so heavy she had to remind herself to breathe while she sat quietly waiting. She couldn't imagine why he had contacted her after all this time, she didn't really have much of material value. Her life was full of promise for the first time since a few days before her sixteenth birthday, but the things she held dear wouldn't be of any value to him. The men flanking her held her heart in their hands, the friends she'd made at the Prairie Winds Club had become her family, what could she have that he would want?

"You are thinking so hard, but you shouldn't. I don't want anything but to get to know you." He took a deep breath and looked at her, and despite her best intentions, Regi felt the connection all the way to the depths of her soul. "I don't deserve it. I certainly haven't earned it, but that doesn't stop me from wanting it with every breath I take."

Regi had never really considered herself a forgiving person. She knew she *should be*, but her aversion to being stung twice by the same bee had often prevented her from going there. *Jesus, peanut butter, and jelly, this would be at least the third sting from the same wasp. What are you thinking setting yourself up for this? But he is the only blood family I have and everyone makes mistakes. Stop being a sap and kick his ass to the curb. But...* Regi's inner battle wasn't making any sense—even to her, and it wasn't resolving anything either. She hadn't even realized she was crying until she heard Kirk's soft curses.

"Come, *anoshi*. Let Brian finish this. You don't have to make a decision right now. Your father has had years to work this through in his mind, you should take your time." She looked up as he pulled her from her chair, the despair in her dad's expression tore at her heart.

"Can you please give Brian your contact information? I...I just need time to think about all of this. I'm not saying no, but I can't say yes either." She was pleased to see the light of hope flicker to life in his eyes as he nodded. She heard the men speaking as Kirk led her from the small building. The last remnants of sunshine were quickly fading and the air had cooled, Kirk held her tucked under his arm as they strolled down the street in companionable silence.

She wasn't sure how far they'd walked when he turned

her so she was facing him, "Listen to your heart, *anoshi*. Let the spirit that lives there lead you."

"I'm trying, but there is so much noise in my head I'm having trouble hearing my heart." She knew that Kirk would understand the spiritual side of her dilemma far better than Brian would. One of the perks of having two men in her life was the way they each seemed to have different strengths that she needed at different times. There were days when Brian's lighthearted way of viewing things was exactly right, but there were so many times Kirk's ability to speak directly to her heart was what grounded her, giving her strength in ways she hadn't known were even possible.

BRIAN SPENT A few minutes listening to Regi's dad lament his actions but wasn't able to work up any real compassion for the man. Even though his entire career was based on being compassionate to those who often deserved it the least, this man had not only gambled with his own life, he'd taken amazing liberties with the lives of the two women he was supposed to love and protect above all others. The Dom in him couldn't imagine how a husband and father had managed to lose both women because of his selfishness. Regi's dad agreed to wait for Regi's call, and Brian had the distinct feeling the man sitting across the table from him wasn't accustomed to waiting for anyone.

Since he and Kirk had worried things might not go perfectly, they'd made a contingency plan that included Kirk escorting Regi out of the café. Brian was relieved to find his friend and their fiancée waiting exactly where he expected to find them. When he pulled up beside them, he saw her surprised expression morph into a knowing grin just before she leaned over and kissed Kirk on the cheek. He rolled down the window and taunted her, "Hey, what was that about? He makes you walk several blocks in those killer heels, I come along to rescue those dainty feet and *he* gets the kiss? That's just wrong." Regi looked up at him and scrambled quickly in beside him, wrapping her arms around his neck and pressing her lips against his. Brian let her have control for a few seconds before he pulled it back firmly and ravaged her mouth with his own. The sweet taste of the tea she'd been drinking lingered along with the intoxicating taste of need.

When Brian finally pulled his lips back from hers, he couldn't hold back his smile. "That dazed expression is every Dom's dream, sweetness. And if we don't get you home right away, I'm not going to be responsible for my actions."

"Yeah, I don't really think the local cops are going to be as understanding about public play as we're accustomed to." Kirk's amusement was easy to hear as he slid in and closed the door. "I'm all over the plan to get our woman home. I think we can order in dinner and see what we can do to turn this evening around." Brian didn't need to be told twice, he helped Kirk fasten Regi's seatbelt and then focused his attention on the road—if the traffic gods managed to work a little of their magic, they might have her naked and between them within a half hour. He had to shift to relieve some of the pressure as his cock hardened even more at the thought of what they had planned for tonight. Brian placed his hand on Regi's knee just as Kirk did the same on her other side. They both pulled so she was open to their touch. Since they hadn't allowed her to keep the panties she'd tried to wear, her sweet scent wafted up to taunt him quickly. He moved both hands back to the steering wheel fearing the first touch would send them right off the edge of the road. Savoring the sweet scent of her arousal was torture and his hands tightened on the steering wheel until his knuckles were white. *Yep, gonna be a very long trip home.*

Chapter Eighteen

TRISH PARKED HER small car along the side of the large parking area so she'd be able to make a quicker exit if this evening didn't go well. She knew the side gate wouldn't be as closely monitored as the other exits because there weren't any outside activities posted for tonight. *Thank you whoever is OCD about that damned website schedule.* She'd been lost in thought as she made her way up the front step and hadn't been paying attention until she heard Trac Hughes' deep voice in front of her as she stepped in the club's reception area. She stepped up close behind him in an effort to avoid Peter Weston's intense stare. She'd heard too much about the Dom who was supposedly some sort of psychic to want him looking her over. *Just what I fucking need, him poking his nose inside my head and setting off every alarm in the place.*

Something was definitely up this evening, people weren't in their usual places and the erotic energy that usually greeted her had been replaced by a nervous anxiety that made her twitch. She didn't consider herself particularly gifted, but the entire atmosphere of the club was so different it was impossible to miss. Trish scooted around behind the men, slid her membership card through the reader while the giant behind the desk was distracted, and quickly made her way into the dressing room. *Thank God Regi isn't here, that bitch never misses anything.* She was grateful Tank had been busy buzzing Trac and Peter through the locked door leading to the club's offices.

Trish hadn't ever been in any of the offices, her interview had taken place in the club's main room. She had learned later that wasn't the way it was usually done and had often wondered why she hadn't been allowed in Kyle and Kent's office. Shaking off the feeling of isolation she always got before the slow slide into darkness. Trish refocused her attention on the task at hand as she slipped the sheathed knife into the top of her boot. She didn't necessarily plan to kill the bitch that had stolen her men, but she wasn't particularly opposed to the idea either.

PETER STOOD TO the side in the West brothers' office and listened as Trac Hughes explained his part in the FBI's investigation of Senator John Stevens. The man clearly didn't like Stevens, but he was also adamant the prick seemed desperate to renew his relationship with Ms. Lanham. Trac agreed with the other members of the security team, it seemed unlikely Stevens was responsible for anything other than ordering his chief of security to watch Meri.

Dex leaned forward resting his forearms on his knees, grinning, "You deliberately botched the installation didn't you?"

"Yeah and I erased most of the footage too." He looked between Dex and Ash, "You two are a couple of ruthless bastards, damn." It didn't take a genius to figure out Meri's assessment of the agent's body language had been correct, the man was definitely a Dom. Hughes' grin and soft chuckle gave away the fact he'd known exactly what had been taking place before any of them had spotted the equipment. Peter didn't feel any deception from the agent, and was relieved to know pictures from the erotic scene hadn't made their way into John Stevens' hands. Peter could feel Trac's disdain for the man he was investigating and couldn't have agreed more.

Ever since the undercover agent had walked in the front door, Peter had felt unsettled, like he'd missed something important. Since the feeling persisted, he quietly excused himself making his way back to the front. Tank was deliberately holding people up as long as possible until he returned, but Peter noticed a short list of members that had already moved into the club. Glancing down he only noted one female member that was unescorted by a Dominant. Since everyone felt they were looking for a woman, hers was the name that caught his eye. "Tank, did you see Trish Jantz arrive?"

"Nope, but I saw her name on the list when I double checked the electronic sign in list, so I wrote her down. When members slide their card through the reader it notes the date and time of their arrival, so I'd say she came in about the same time you went down the hall with Mr. Hughes." Tank was aptly named because the man was absolutely enormous. It wasn't hard to see him as the professional football player he'd once been. What did blindside most people was the fact he was extremely bright. He worked at Prairie Winds because he liked the people, not because he had an interest in the lifestyle or needed the money. From what Peter had heard, Tank had invested the money he'd earned playing for the Cowboys rather than indulging in the extravagant lifestyle most professional athletes enjoy. After his last closed head trauma, the man had made the wise decision to walk away, and thanks to his foresight, had been financially able to do so.

MERI LEANED AGAINST the railing surrounding the pool area and looked out over the beautifully landscaped gardens spread out like a Victorian era fan beginning at the front of the Prairie Winds Forum Shops. The forum shops were Tobi and Gracie's pet project. The convenience and privacy of having quality fetish clothing and supplies readily available meant the small shops had been a re-sounding success. Most members of the club living the BDSM lifestyle had careers where preserving their reputa-tions was paramount, so having a *safe* place to shop was a huge plus for them. And the added bonus of having specialty personal services available meant Doms could now personally supervise their subs during their waxing or massage settings without the technicians freaking out.

During a recent gab session, Tobi had admitted family friend, Cameron Barnes, was trying to enlist their help to set up something similar at his ultra-exclusive club in Houston. Tobi and Gracie were both excited about the opportunity, but admitted their men were less thrilled. *It'll be interesting to see how that plays out.* Tobi must have noticed how Meri had stiffened when she and Gracie had mentioned their men weren't sold on the idea, because she quickly explained, "They don't want us taking on too much since we both have small children to care for, you know how overly protective they tend to be. We teased them that they are just worried they won't get as much nookie as they do now."

"You should have seen their expressions. Holy Mother

of God in heaven, I don't think they'd even considered that angle. A couple of them actually went pale." Gracie broke out in gales of laughter at the memory and Meri had felt herself relax when she'd realized the women weren't offended by their men's concerns. She wished she knew their secret. Their self-confidence was inspiring. Why couldn't she get the memories of John Stevens' words to stop playing over and over like a stuck record in her head? Being called stupid by someone who was obviously less intelligent was annoying enough, but realizing she'd actually entertained the idea his words might be valid was just plain exasperating.

She wondered if there were programs to help women identify emotional abuse and combat its long-term effects. She knew the local shelter worked extensively with domestic violence victims, but there had to be many victims whose injuries were from words not fists...who helped them? Meri thought back over all the times John had screamed at her that she was worthless and stupid, and held them up against the day-to-day interactions she'd seen between her parents. Her mom and dad had been her biggest supporters, they'd always encouraged her to stretch her wings and to try the very things that scared her. If she didn't want to pursue the activities, that was her decision...as long as she'd given it a fair shot before quitting. Her dad had arranged music lessons, mercy had that ever been a bust. Her mom...painting and sculpture lessons at a local gallery. Those had gone marginally better, but it had been clear to everyone the arts probably weren't going to be her life's passion.

Meri had learned to swim, tried ballroom dancing, and various sports, but nothing had really captured her interest. It wasn't until her dad introduced her to martial arts that she'd felt as if she'd finally found her niche. Her mom had been mortified by the bruises she'd gotten in the beginning, but had quickly realized how valuable the skills would be. Knowing her daughter could easily fend off most attackers had quieted her mother's protests. Meri still trained as often as she could, and even though her skills were no longer sharp enough for competition, she wasn't a lightweight when it came to protecting herself either.

The night air sent a chill up her spine, fall had definitely arrived. A light breeze sent chill bumps racing over her skin and Meri wondered how long she'd been outside. Ash and Dex had been meeting with Special Agent Hughes for so long she'd gotten tired of waiting inside and had stepped out for a few moments of peace and quiet. When she turned to walk back inside, she came face to face with a young woman whose sneering expression caused her to take a step back. The brunette was dressed in clothing befitting a submissive, but her body language wasn't right for the part. Recovering, Meri moved forward and attempted to step around the woman saying, "Excuse me."

"I don't fucking think so, bitch. I've waited months for this moment. Don't move." The woman's eyes were wild with a crazed anger Meri didn't understand, but the hint of insanity was easy to figure out! Meri stepped back another step and felt the edge of the pool beneath her bare feet. Letting her eyes move over the woman in front of her, she wanted to smile when she noticed her assailant's ill-fitting thigh high leather boots. *Oh yeah, those babies are going to fill with water and you'll sink like a stone. Now to figure out how to get her crazy ass in the pool.*

Meri subtly slid her foot along the edge of the smooth concrete making sure she was in the best possible position. One of the points her self-defense instructors had driven home time and again was the importance of knowing everything you could about your environment and position before engaging. "Who are you?"

The woman's eyes narrowed and Meri found herself wondering what she could have done to make her so angry. Even though she'd seen the young woman at the club, Meri was certain she hadn't ever met the woman personally. "You don't know me?" she asked. Before Meri could respond, the woman huffed in exasperation, "Of course you don't, you're too important to bother with the likes of me." Meri didn't take her eyes off the woman's face, but could see her rolling the handle of a long, slender knife against her palm, it was that nervous gesture that told Meri just how unstable her assailant was. An angry attacker was much more predictable than one who was skating on the edge of crazy...*and leave it to me to get some whack-job who wants to knife me by a pool...on a cool fall evening...outside a kink club. Lord of the Lepers, my life is a Charles Dickens' novel parody. Great headlines—I can see it now—Local Foundation Leader Makes Huge Splash in Attack Outside Local Sex Club. Oh yes, indeed—the local gossip columnists and tabloids will have a field day with this one.*

"I know you are a member of the club, but I don't think we've ever been introduced. Care to enlighten me about this..." Meri said as she waved her hand in the direction of the knife the woman was holding. "It seems to me that I should at least have the opportunity to know why you're so angry."

"They were supposed to be mine...they said they were coming back for me, but they didn't. They took you to the dungeon instead. I watched you know...I watched them whip you. I knew it was a punishment, but everyone could see when it changed. Everybody talked about it, the uncollared subs were practically swooning." Meri was baffled—did Ash and Dex have some connection to this woman? Had they been in a relationship with her? Holy shit, she *did not* want to get involved in a domestic disturbance and this woman sounded as if she had some claim to the men. *Hell, the headlines are getting juicier by the minute.*

Stall. It was the only thing Meri knew to do. She was unarmed and the crazy woman in front of her was becoming more agitated with each breath she took. *Maybe John was right, my kinks will cause me nothing but trouble...because it sure seems to be playing out that way...well, that isn't entirely true...there have been some pretty spectacular moments...but even those aren't worth the price I'm paying. If I get out of this unscathed, I'll walk away, and chalk it all up to learning experience.* Just thinking about walking away from Dex and Ash sent shards of pain through her chest, Meri felt her entire body clench at the thought. *No...focus on this moment...don't be distracted or you'll miss that microsecond of opportunity to make your move.*

MICAH PUT OUT the alert as soon as the silent door alarms sounded. Whoever had attempted to lock up the system hadn't known about the back-ups, so he'd unlocked all the doors with the flip of a switch. There had only been one blind spot on the Prairie Winds property and it had been Lilly West who'd discovered it. She'd exploited the information and shared it with the women months earlier, but they'd quickly remedied the problem so he should be able to see every nook and cranny of the entire property. As he scanned the monitors he noted the feed from one of the pool's cameras was blurred out. He immediately entered the commands to begin recording, but it took several seconds to move other cameras into position so they displayed that area. As things came into focus, what he saw nearly stole his breath.

Meri was backed up to the pool and even though she was looking at the woman in front of her, Micah noticed her furtive glances to the camera above the woman's head. He knew she would have no way of knowing that wasn't the one she needed to play to, but he was grateful she was focused enough to know where to look for help. He sent out the all-call and then began listening to their conversation.

"They were mine before you came along. I'd played their game and had them eating out of the palm of my hand. Hell, you can go back to that ass-wipe boss of mine anytime you want to, so it's not like you won't have a man." The woman's shrill laugh reminded Micah of fingernails against a blackboard and the grating sound made her shudder.

"You work for John? Did he send you here?" If Micah hadn't been a trained sexual Dominant he might have missed the mixed tones of Meri's voice. It was clear she was waffling between fear and anger, and he'd be willing to bet anger was going to quickly win out.

"Yes and no. I have worked for him since just after you two broke up. It was easy to land the job, I just had to make myself look like you." Micah saw Meri's eyes widen as she realized just how true the woman's statement had been. Zooming in closer with another camera, Micah was surprised to see the two women did bear a striking resemblance to one another. "I'm finished working for him, but I assure you he isn't finished paying me." Meri looked as puzzled by that statement as Micah felt and the woman he'd just identified as Trish Jantz, was happy to continue even as she stepped forward and waved the knife at Meri. "I've got enough on that worm to keep him paying my way for a good long while. And when I've bled him dry, I'll go after his business associates because I've compiled some nice tidbits on several of them as well. But that isn't why I'm here." The woman leaned forward and sneered, "You're a hard woman to scare off, and I'm ready to ensure you stay away from my men from now on." *Her men? Is she talking about Ash and Dex? What the hell?*

During Micah's career as a Special Forces operative, he'd seen missions go completely to hell in the blink of an eye on several occasions, but he'd never seen a clusterfuck unfold as quickly as the one on the screen directly in front of him. Somewhere in the back of his mind the thought raced through his mind that he'd have to play this back in slow motion to see everything because there was no way to process the explosion of activity playing out down by the pool.

Chapter Nineteen

A SH AND DEX were both still in the Wests' office even though their meeting had technically ended. They'd been offering their assistance to Special Agent Hughes when the first security alerts vibrated their phones. Since they'd left Meri at the bar with instructions to wait for them to return for her, they weren't worried she was the woman they were rushing to help. But the second alert pinged their phones before they'd made their way out the back of the club, and hearing Micah's sit-rep identifying Meri as the woman being accosted had sent a white-hot bolt of fear racing up Ash's spine. "Did he say Trish Jantz?" When Dex merely nodded, he continued, "What the hell does she want with Meri?" Even as the words were leaving his mouth, he knew the answer.

He and Dex had agreed to scene with the young woman the night they'd met Meri despite their mutual reluctance to do so. They'd known she was becoming too attached, but had fooled themselves into believing one more scene wouldn't matter. Neither of them had ever figured out how she'd managed to get their personal cell phone numbers, but the deluge of text messages they'd received had become more and more aggressive as the weeks wore on. Both of them had recently blocked her number in hopes of sending a clear message. Ordinarily they'd have confronted her face to face, but protecting

Meri had become their priority and they simply hadn't taken time to follow through. The truth was it had probably been far too easy to simply let the problem slide and now it seemed Meri was paying the piper.

Ash burst through the gated area surrounding the pool just as both women screamed and hit the water at the deep end of the pool. Dex, Trac, and Peter were right behind him, and before he could kick off his boots, both women had sunk to the bottom. They were struggling and Ash saw a reflection from the underwater lights glint off shiny steel blade of a knife. In his peripheral vision, Ash saw Dex ridding himself of his boots and they hit the water at the same time.

The pool wasn't particularly large, but it was fairly deep. It only took the former SEALs a few short strokes to reach the women and he'd been stunned to see Mary grab the back of Trish's shirt and push off the bottom toward the surface. Since he was closest to the bitch who'd attacked Meri, he took over and was surprised at how difficult she was to maneuver through the water. *God damned boots have to be full of water, no wonder she went straight to the bottom.*

Trish was unconscious but still breathing when Trac and Peter pulled her out of the water. Dex helped Meri to the edge before climbing out quickly. Ash watched his friend lean forward, wrap his hands around Meri's forearms, and effortlessly lift her from the water. It was only then that Ash noticed the trail of pink tinging the pool water.

Meri's clothes were plastered against her tan skin making it difficult to see where she was hurt. Ash left Trish to the others, focusing on Meri, "Is she hurt?" Ash saw her eyes flame for just a second as she realized he directed his question to Dex rather than her, but just as she opened her mouth to protest her knees folded out from under her and she dropped like a stone.

MERI'S LUNGS FELT like they were going to burst as she fought the crazy bitch who'd stabbed her. She hadn't been able to take a deep breath before they'd gone under and for a few seconds she'd wondered if they weren't both going to drown. Just as she'd predicted, the woman's boots had instantly filled with water and taken her straight to the bottom of the pool. What Meri hadn't counted on was the woman's panic. The loony broad had latched on to Meri and fought so hard Meri hadn't been able to get her back to the top before the crazy woman passed out. Just as she'd pushed off the bottom toward the surface, someone had pulled the woman from her hold. It was then that she'd felt a band of steel encircle her waist. She was propelled toward the surface by whoever was holding her, and she was grateful because her lungs burned as if they'd been set on fire.

At the pool's edge her rescuer had placed her hands atop one another and climbed effortlessly from the water. Strong hands had wrapped around her arms and lifted her to the pool deck in one swift movement. The sudden jolt sent a white-hot bolt of pain through her chest that had actually dimmed her vision for several seconds before the gray dissipated enough for her to see Ash and Dex. When she'd tried to take a breath another lancing pain rioted through her chest and the sensation of falling and encroaching darkness warred with one another before she let go and slid silently into the peaceful abyss.

DEX HAD ONLY been a half step behind Ash, but it had felt like a mile. He'd been kicking off his own boots before he'd even stopped running. The pool was fairly deep and swimming those few feet to the bottom had seemed to take forever. By the time he'd wrapped his arm around Meri's waist the adrenaline flooding his system had caused him to band her too tightly to his side and he felt her jolt at the pressure. It had been easy to lift her out of the pool with his arms held straight out in front of him and he'd seen her eyes go wide in surprise. When he'd pulled her against his chest she'd cried out in pain, then setting her back on her feet he'd heard Ash ask if she was hurt just before she collapsed. He'd caught her easily, but had to fight the rising tide of panic sweeping through him when he realized the gap at the front of his black leather vest was smeared with blood.

Dex heard Ash speaking to their former teammates and for just a moment he felt as if they were back in some hellhole on the other side of the globe. But the fragile woman lying on the smooth concrete in front of him brought him fully back to the moment. He made quick work of shredding the thin chemise they'd let her wear to the club. Since that was all she was wearing she lay bare on the quickly cooling concrete in under a second. She had one stab wound to the chest that was bleeding heavily. It wasn't pumping blood out and he let out an audible sigh of relief because the wound had to be perilously close to her heart. Watching her chest closely he noticed she seemed to be struggling to breathe. Running his hands over her tan skin he noticed it was turning an odd shade of blue, when he found the bubbling wound on her right side he knew why. "She's taken one to the right lung." He didn't need to say any more, he just held out his hand knowing one of his teammates would provide what he needed.

Dex covered both wounds with clean towels from a nearby cabinet, applying enough pressure to her side that Meri moaned in pain without ever surfacing from the darkness that had claimed her. Kent West tucked one of the soft subbie blankets around her lower half and Dex appreciated his friend's concern for her modesty. Even though they were in a kink club, and as Doms they were all accustomed to enjoying the view of naked women, the ambulance crew that was no doubt on their way was going to be another story. Dex quickly looked her over before saying, "There are several lacerations on her arms, but none of them seem serious. How far out is the ambulance?"

Kyle stepped up in front on Meri's other side and answered, "Their ETA was ten a couple of minutes ago." Just as he finished speaking, they heard a scream from the balcony above them followed immediately by a door slamming. "Fuck, get ready. She'll have called in the reinforcements by the time she hits the back door. I swear I'd pocket her damned cell phone but we've got a tracker in it." Dex braced himself for the tiny blonde tornado that was Tobi West.

"I thought the tracker was in her collar?" Dex knew Ash had asked the question more as a distraction than because he needed the information.

"There too, but it seems our lovely wife has figured out a way to jam the signals coming from her jewelry—we still don't know exactly how she's managing it, but she never goes anywhere without that damned phone because of the kids, so we tagged it. You'd think my brother and I were incapable of caring for our own children the way she calls home every half hour."

The wail of a siren began filling the quiet evening just as Tobi stormed into the pool area asking questions so quickly Dex had no idea how Kent and Kyle kept up. It was easy to see it took them both to stay ahead of the petite whirlwind. But even as she was rattling off questions at a lightning pace, she was smoothing Meri's hair away from her face with gentle sweeps of her fingers. When Kent started to pull her to her feet, Tobi leaned forward and brushed a kiss over Meri's forehead, "You better be alright or I'm going to be very pissed...and I'm a real pain in the ass when I'm mad."

"Kitten," Kyle's stern warnings to his sweet wife about her cursing were so common that most of the other Doms rarely even noticed any more.

"See what you've done? I'm going to be in trouble because of this, so now you're obligated to recover quickly." When she looked up at Dex, her sweet face was filled with a level of fear and anguish that squeezed Dex's heart. Tobi West might not be the perfect submissive, but she had a heart the size of Texas, and knowing her background made that fact even more remarkable.

Standing back watching the first responders care for Meri was one of the hardest things Dex had ever done. It didn't seem to matter if a SEAL was active or retired, apparently the desire to *act* was imprinted on their DNA. Dex noticed the same restless energy seemed to be almost pulsing from Ash as well. The man was practically bouncing on the balls of his feet and Dex didn't think he'd ever seen Ash so unhinged. The few minutes the attendants spent stabilizing Meri seemed like hours. Just as they lifted her onto the gurney, she began gasping for air and Dex knew her lung had fully collapsed. He'd seen it in the field and knew the terror she had to be feeling. Everyone around them tried to calm her, but it had been he and Ash's barked commands that had finally settled her. Her eyes had briefly fluttered open and instead of fear, Dex had seen sadness and loss. They'd moved her away so quickly he hadn't gotten the chance to reassure her that they wouldn't leave her side, and something deep in his soul told him it was a missed opportunity he was going to regret.

MERI FELT LIKE she'd run a 5K race in lead boots. She couldn't open her eyes but that didn't keep her from sweeping her hands up in an attempt to remove the concrete block someone had set on her chest. "No, baby, you have to leave the tubes in for a bit longer." *Mom? Tubes? Why is mom in my room? And why is there so much noise? I'm so tired...* The quiet of sleep lured her back into its peaceful darkness, but just before she slid beneath the cloak of silence, she remembered how her heart had been shattered. The men she'd grown to trust had another woman, one who had stabbed her before Meri had plunged them both into the cool water of the Wests' swimming pool. How had she not known? Why hadn't she at least asked if they were involved with someone else? Was this just another case of men pretending to be interested in her because of her parents' money? *Too many questions. I'll worry about it later.*

The next time Meri awoke the room she was sleeping in was quiet except for the soft beeping she recognized as a heart monitor. It took several seconds for her eyes to focus and her mind to clear enough for her to realize she was in a hospital room. Before she'd even had a chance to speak, cool fingers brushed her hair aside. When she turned her head, Tobi's sweet face smiled down at her, "Welcome back, sweetie. We've been waiting for you to wake up. Everybody finally went downstairs to get something to eat, so it's just you and me for a few minutes. I'll give you a fast update before they return if you want me to. Do you need a drink?"

Meri managed to nod and got several big gulps of water down before Tobi pulled the straw back from her lips. "Whoa there, sister. Mercy, you trying to get me in Dutch with the heinous bitch taking care of you? Holy horny toads, if there was ever a woman who needed to get laid, its Nurse Wicked." Tobi giggled and when Meri started to laugh she cried out at the stabbing pain in her side. "Damn, you probably don't want to do that again, huh? I'll try not to be so entertaining, but I'm warning you it really does just sort of come naturally." Patting the side of her hair with her hand, she grinned, "Just like Lucy Van Pelt, I think I'm pretty special...even though my Charlie Brown and Snoopy might argue the point." The sudden horrified look on Tobi's face made Meri worry before she quickly added, "Damnation. I'm talking like the mother of toddlers. Oh my God, I swear I'm going to call Cam this afternoon and make arrangements to go down and work at his club in Houston. I need adult conversation and helping his staff setup his shops gives Gracie and I *both* an opportunity to remember there is life outside of Toddlerville."

Meri wasn't sure if it was the medication or Tobi's usual rapid-fire topic changes, but she was having trouble keeping up and it must have shown in her expression. "Oh dear, I'm doing it again. Oh well, here's the scoop before the troops storm the walls and I get pushed back by those men of yours." Meri felt her eyes fill with tears at Tobi's words. How was she going to tell her friend that the men working for her husband had another woman? "What's wrong, honey? You look like somebody ran over your puppy. Are you in pain? I can call Nurse Ratched if you need her."

"No, please, go on, but don't call them mine, okay?" Tobi's eyes filled with confusion and concern for a few seconds before she shrugged her shoulders and proceeded to update Meri on everything that had happened during the time she'd been out. Meri was relieved to find out her parents had already been on their way home and that she hadn't been asleep long enough for them to travel all the way from South America.

By the time everyone returned, Meri realized how lucky she'd been because the wound to her chest had missed her heart by less than a quarter inch. Seeing the lines of strain around her mom's and dad's eyes made Meri wish she could hug them close and assure them she was fine, but just being awake was draining her energy, within minutes she felt her eye lids edging south. Dex and Ash walked in the room just as she gave up the battle, the last thing she remembered was them pressing soft kisses against her brow and sweet assurances that she was going to be fine. *No promises that they'll be around...but then why did I think they would?*

Chapter Twenty

Two Weeks Later

TOBI SQUIRMED IN her seat and studied her fingers as they clenched and unclenched the silky fabric of the dress she was wearing. Bright morning sunlight streamed through her husbands' floor to ceiling office windows making her feel as though she was under a giant spotlight. Tobi was barely able to keep from swinging her legs back and forth above the polished wood floor—*damn I hate being short*—but it would have just been nervous energy since the little-girl-lost routine only worked when she was alone with her husbands and right now there were four very pissed off Doms studying her. *I feel like a damn lab rat.* Their laser-like gazes were probably going to have her bursting into flames any minute and that might be a better end than the one she'd be facing when they found out the truth.

She'd actually been expecting this confrontation ever since she and Gracie had returned from Houston. Neither of them had intended to introduce CeCe Barnes to Meri, but the sweet surgeon had walked into the small deli where the three of them had been eating lunch, so introducing the two women had been unavoidable. CeCe was married to Cameron Barnes, the club owner she and Gracie were helping, she was also his full-time slave outside of her career. Kyle had once said that CeCe embraced the lifestyle with "everything in her" which Tobi knew was code for "she's a good sub, you could learn from her". Of course Tobi hadn't been able to keep that opinion to herself and she'd gotten a sound spanking that hadn't really been much of a deterrent for her bratty behavior.

"Kitten, I asked you a question." Kyle wasn't fooling her, she knew that tone of voice and it was pure deception. *Geez, I hope I don't look that dim-witted.*

"Um, sorry, guess I was daydreaming. Could you refresh my memory?" *Holy shades of pissed off, did they all four just growl in unison? Pretty sure that isn't a good sign.* Any hope she'd had of bullshitting her way out of her current predicament evaporated into a puff of smoke when she heard the side door open and watched Peter step through. Meeting his gaze, she didn't even try to hold back her groan. Looking back at the four men facing her she wanted to slap the self-satisfied smiles right off their faces.

"That isn't fair you know."

"It wouldn't be an issue if you were planning to tell the truth, now would it?" Kent wasn't usually the snarky one and on the rare occasions he was less than charming, she was usually up to her ass in alligators.

"Kitten? I'll ask you again, mostly for Peter's benefit since I know full well you remember the question. Do you know where Merilee Lanham is?"

"Well fuck a fat leprechaun."

"Tobi." Kyle's growled warning about her language had more bite than usual. *Probably gonna pay big time for that one.*

"Well...sort of."

Kyle, Kent, Dex, and Ash all four glared at her, Peter was the only one who grinned. Shaking his head, he leaned over from the seat he'd taken beside her and whispered conspiratorially, "They're gonna make you walk the plank if you don't come clean, sweet wench." His pirate reference might not have made much sense to the other men in the room, but it told Tobi that he knew exactly where Meri was because Cam's club was hosting a pirate themed party tonight.

"Drat. I promised. It's not nice to make people break their promises." When none of them even blinked, she sighed and started talking. By the time she'd finished, Kent was already on the phone making arrangements for his parents' private jet to take his friends to Houston. When she slid her hand into her pocket, Peter wrapped his hand around her wrist.

"Hand your phone to me, sweetness. I'm sure your Masters will see to it you get it back first thing tomorrow." When she rolled her eyes, he narrowed his. "Be very careful, little one, I am not the pushover you think I am. At the end of the day I am still a Dom, and rolling your eyes at any Dom is never a good idea."

His tone alone would have been enough to stop her cold, but the words had also held a hint of disappointment, and one of the things Tobi always responded to. She might not be a perfect sub, but she was definitely submissive. Pleasing others was at the core of her nature and she felt bad knowing she'd lowered his opinion of her. He used his fingers to raise her chin so she was forced to look into his brilliant green eyes. "Don't go there, sweetie. The next time you're getting a good thrashing out in the Woodshed, I'll get in a couple of swats and we'll call it even."

"Yes, Sir." *I hope you find a sub for yourself real soon...maybe you'll forget...but what woman will ever stand a chance if you know everything they're thinking?*

He grinned and leaned closer to whisper, "I can't hear

everyone you know. And my granny always said I'd know I'd found the right woman when I couldn't *cheat* by using my gifts." Peter pulled her to her feet before reaching down to tap the tip of her nose. When she blinked up at him, he tossed her phone onto Kyle's desk and walked out of the room. She had almost relaxed when she turned and saw Kyle standing in front of her with his arms crossed and his legs spread apart in the stance every submissive she knew recognized as trouble.

When Kent stepped up alongside his brother and adopted a similar stance, Tobi actually started to step back until Kent spoke, "Don't you dare." He looked at Kyle and continued, "The dads are on their way to pick up the kids." When Tobi started to speak, he shifted his gaze to her, "Not. One. Word. You know perfectly well why we didn't call mom, she'd tip off Meri just as you had planned to do. Dad Dell has already secured her phone and Jax has Gracie's, so you should just as well stop trying to figure out a way to dig yourself any deeper." His words sounded harsh, but there was a twinkle in his eyes that told her things weren't going to be as bad as she'd feared. Tobi let out the breath she hadn't even realized she was hold-ing...just before he said, "Strip." *Oh boy.*

MERI STOOD IN front of the enormous windows of her parents' Houston condo and looked out over the glistening waters of the Gulf of Mexico without really seeing any-thing. Ordinarily she considered the view breathtaking, but today she longed to be home. Her parents had chosen the perfect location to build the home she'd grown up in. The mansion set on the edge of the river headwaters that quickly became Lake Travis. She'd grown up appreciating the fact she had the best of both worlds right out her front door. Their elderly groundskeeper had taken time to teach her how to fish along the banks of the river and her dad had introduced her to the joys of sailing on the large lake.

Melancholy swamped her, threatening to pull her under in a riptide of despair. She'd truly believed the day she'd been dismissed from the hospital was the worst day of her life, but each day since had been just as devastating. Thinking back to how it had felt to look up from the wheelchair she'd been forced to use into Dex's and Ash's bewildered expressions after she'd said her safe word threatened to shatter her heart yet again. The looks on their faces had been a mixture of shock and fury, but in the end they'd both stepped back and watched silently as she'd settled in the back of her father's car. She'd cried all the way to the airport and openly sobbed during the entire flight to Houston. Heck, she'd cried so much she had worried she was going to turn into a raisin.

She hadn't expected the heart wrenching loneliness to build stronger rather than abate. *Shows what all those damned poets know.* The time she'd spent with Tobi and Gracie had been a blessed distraction, but now that they'd both returned to Prairie Winds, the silence surrounding her was deafening. Her friends had assured her Ash and Dex had not *belonged* to Trish Jantz and that listening to a "fruit cake" was ridiculous, but the fact the men hadn't even attempted to find her seemed to speak clearly enough.

Tobi had rattled on that neither man had expressed any interest in the woman now sitting in the Travis County Jail—where she was likely to spend a very long time. The Lanham Foundation's team of lawyers was working alongside Noelle Chambers who was a club member and a prosecutor. Meri had to smile thinking about how much things had changed. Noelle had come into the bathroom while Kelly had been spewing vile sludge at Tobi. Meri had been a reluctant accomplice and had taken the punishment Ash and Dex had doled out. Maybe it was karma that she'd ended up dating John Stevens because being on the receiving end of verbal abuse had made Meri even more remorseful for her part in hurting Tobi.

Turning to see the white box that had been delivered just after lunch, Meri sighed and tried to imagine going to the club owned by her new friend's husband. She'd met CeCe Barnes when Tobi and Gracie had finally dragged her out to lunch. CeCe was incredible—warm, open, brilliant, and clearly devoted to her Master and their baby girl, Chloe. When she'd invited Meri to visit the club, Meri hadn't taken the invitation seriously, assuming it had simply been a social nicety. But the beautiful box that had arrived earlier had contained a lovely printed note from CeCe with a handwritten postscript from her husband. From what Meri had heard from Tobi and Gracie, Cameron Barnes was not a man to be ignored. Both women liked and respected him, but they'd also mentioned several times he was the very definition of Dominant.

Flipping the lid off and pulling back the tissue, Meri ran her fingers slowly over the silk and lace wench's costume. The green was the same shade as the one she'd been wearing the night she'd been stabbed, but instead of dredging up fear, it only intensified her feeling of loss. Had she made a mistake walking away? Was it possible Tobi was right and Trish Jantz had been exaggerating her connection with the men Meri had fallen for? *Damn it, I wasn't supposed to fall in love with them. I knew better…*

Picking up the small parchment note, Meri re-read the

short note at the bottom:

> *I will send a car for you at nine p.m. Wait in the safety of your home until the driver calls for you. Wear the gift we've sent under a coat and shoes you can slip off easily. A member of my staff will meet you at the door with further instructions. —Master C—*

Wasn't it just like a Dom to write a note full of instructions and totally lacking in any finesse. Master C was clearly a man accustomed to being obeyed rather than questioned. He didn't invite, he commanded, and Meri found herself compelled to comply despite that small part of her brain that scrambled to protest. Since she didn't have anything else to do this evening, perhaps it was time to begin reclaiming her life. The doctors were thrilled with her rapid recovery and she'd already been released to do pretty much as she pleased. And truthfully, just thinking about watching another chick flick while vegging out in the media room just might cause her to jump off the balcony.

CAMERON BARNES RUBBED his stinging palm over the burning ass cheeks spread so lusciously over his lap and smiled at his sweet sub's sharp intake of breath. She so rarely misbehaved he'd forgotten now much fun these spontaneous scenes could be. Oh that didn't mean he didn't plan elaborate punishment scenes with his brilliant beauty because he loved punishing her for pleasure, but *this* scene had been a delightful surprise. He continued to squeeze her smarting globes, giving the burn a chance to work its magic before he slid his fingers through the folds of her slick pussy. He knew her body so well he felt the first spasm of the muscles around his fingers, it had been little more than a butterfly's soft flutter but he'd felt it. "Oh no, my mouthy slave, you won't be getting a reward for some time."

Her softly whispered, "Yes, Master," was music to his ears.

"Have you been re-thinking the wisdom of your earlier decision?" Truthfully he'd been thrilled when she'd stormed into his office raving about a message she'd gotten from Merilee Lanham. She'd demanded an explanation and he'd had to suppress his smile as he'd ordered her to strip. For the first time in years she'd actually hesitated several seconds—a decision that was going to cost her several additional swats—but she had finally complied and lowered herself over his knees. Cam hadn't spared her and the first slaps had left perfect imprints of his hand on each side of her ivory ass.

"Yes, Master…but." *Smart subbie, but a bit too late.* He rained down several more blows spreading them over her ass and thighs.

"Try again."

"Yes, Master. I'm sorry, Master." The tremor in her voice let him know she was crying softly—God, CeCe cried more beautifully than any other woman he'd ever known. No swollen eyes or red nose for his slave, she reminded him of a Victorian debutante when she dabbed away her tears with the lacy handkerchiefs she always seemed to have within reach.

"Good. We'll discuss this as soon as we're finished, because I do believe you've earned several more swats for your hesitance to remove your clothing." Pulling open his desk drawer he grabbed the flexible fiberglass ruler he knew would leave lovely welts that she'd carry into next week as reminders of tonight's lesson. CeCe wasn't a masochist so he was careful to make sure the level of pain was appropriate for the lesson. He didn't want to entirely suppress her sass because that would only deny him future opportunities like this one. His lovely slave enjoyed erotic pain, but she'd be reminded each time she sat down for the next several days that she'd crossed the line of respect tonight.

After laying five perfectly parallel lines across her ass he dropped the ruler on the desk and pushed his fingers deep into her fluttering vagina. Just as she was nearing the edge of release he pulled back and positioned her over the desk. "Open everything to my view, pet." She was positively glorious, and by the time her foggy mind processed his command he would have his throbbing cock in hand and ready to sink deep. His only worry was that his *need* was going to trump his infamous *control*. The little minx had lit a fuse he worried was going to burn far too quickly.

Looking down at her lying naked with her small hands pulling her sore ass cheeks wide for his pleasure, Cam couldn't help the small bit of regret that he could no longer keep her naked all the time at home. She'd rarely been allowed any type of clothing in their home—even during her pregnancy. But now that they had a full-time live-in nanny, they'd had to make some changes that neither one enjoyed. He was actively looking for a nanny who was in the lifestyle, because he missed having her body available to him all the time. It had taken Dr. Cecelia Barnes time to accept her desire to submit, the professional who'd fought her way to the upper echelons of pediatric surgery had narrowed her self-view until she'd forgotten she was a woman with strong sexual needs. She'd told him one night after a particularly intense session the most precious gift he'd ever given her was her sexuality. He'd brushed her sweat-dampened hair from her eyes and shaken his head, "No, my love, it was always right at your fingertips, I simply helped you grasp it."

Glancing toward the large clock above the fireplace in his office, Cam quickly calculated exactly how much time he had to enjoy her before duty called. Pushing himself slowly through her swollen tissues, Cam smiled at the wet sounds. The smell of her desire had filled the room seconds after he'd begun spanking her, and seeing her cream coating his cock kicked his control a little bit closer to the edge. Pushing in again ever so slowly before pulling out against the clenching muscles of her sex was erotic torture so sweet Cam felt his knees begin to weaken. God in heaven what was it about this one woman that leveled him?

Concentrating on the plans he'd made for her was his only hope at distracting himself. Cam mentally reviewed his conversation with his old friend, Jax McDonald, he still wasn't sure how the man had convinced him to become involved when everything about tonight went against his longstanding rule against meddling in the lives of others. Giving himself a mental shake, Cam couldn't help wondering if becoming a father hadn't made him soft. But on the other hand, if everything went according to plan he would score enough points with the Wests that he might get Tobi and Gracie to return for the Grand Opening Gala. He'd already negotiated Gracie's return with Jax in return for his help with Merilee tonight. The work Tobi and Gracie had managed to complete in just one week had been humbling. He and his staff had worked alongside them and they had all been amazed at their knowledge, dedication, and work ethic. *I wonder if their men fully appreciate the resource they have at their fingertips?*

Cam looked down at the gorgeous woman in front of him and felt a surge of protective ownership welling up inside him. CeCe had earned a reputation as one of the leading pediatric surgeons in the nation. Her private clinic brought in patients from all over the world, she was brilliant, kind, and *his*. It wasn't a surprise that CeCe had become fast friends with both Tobi and Gracie because the old adage that said *like attracts like* was certainly true in this instance.

His cock was protesting that he'd stalled long enough, and his brain agreed—it was time to give his beautiful pet what she needed because above all else, she craved his approval. "You have done so well, my love. You accepted your punishment with such dignity and grace." Leaning down so his lips brushed over the shell of her ear, he whispered, "Come for me, love. I want to hear you screaming my name." The intensity of her response was brutal and her scream bounced around the room making him grateful he'd soundproofed his inner sanctum shortly after he'd first met her. *Oh yeah, his lovely slave had a great set of lungs on her.* Her muscles locked down squeezing his cock with enough strength to launch him in blissful oblivion just seconds after she'd crested. The jerking of his cock deep in her and his hot seed shooting against her cervix pushed her back up the mountain of desire and straight into another frenzied orgasm.

Cameron had been forced to lock his knees and lean forward so most of his weight rested on his arms to avoid sliding to the floor. If CeCe ever fully understood the power she held over him, it would tip the balance of their D/s relationship into dangerous territory. In truth, neither of them would be truly happy in a vanilla relationship, it simply wasn't who they were. But the fact she'd challenged him today was a clear indicator that they'd fallen into a rut—it was obviously time to step up his game. If his lovely slave needed more of his attention, then she was damned well going to get it.

Chapter Twenty-One

THE RAP AT her door at precisely nine p.m. startled Meri. She'd expected Master C's driver to call for her from the lobby and the fact he'd made it past the doorman and desk guard indicated just how well connected Cameron Barnes was. Tobi had only given Meri sketchy details about the man, but she wasn't sure if that was all Tobi knew or all she'd been given permission to share. The former Special Forces operative had parlayed his vast military experience into a very lucrative career as a mercenary, but he'd given it up after collaring CeCe. Tobi told her Cameron and Jax's families had been long-time friends, but hadn't explained any further. She hadn't wondered about it before, but now something about that niggled at the back of her mind.

To her surprise, the drive to Dark Desires wasn't a long one. The gated entrance looked like any number of warehouses along the docks at the waterfront. Approaching the large brick building, Meri was surprised to see how effectively the landscaping concealed members from anyone on the street intent on taking pictures with a zoom lens. Obviously this was an exclusive club whose members valued their privacy. The man who opened her door was so good looking, for a moment Meri wondered if he was a model, there was something so familiar about him that her distraction caused her to stumble getting out of the car.

Crap-a-moly…nothing embarrassing about that! She assumed it happened to the young man a lot because he seemed completely unfazed, catching her easily and setting her on her feet.

"Good evening, Ms. Lanham. If you will follow me, Master Cameron is waiting for you in his office." The sandy-haired god whisked her through the front door and Meri suddenly felt as if her feet had been glued to the floor. The large entry was such a shock that she heard herself gasp in surprise. The rich jewel tones and opulent furnishings made her think she'd taken a trip back in time, and she found herself surrounded by the lavish beauty of the late eighteen hundreds. The brocade rugs bore sweeping designs of gold and deep red. The enormous reception desk looked as if it had once been used for hotel registrations. Even the paintings on the wall appeared to be from a time gone by…until you looked closely and realized they were elaborate works of erotic art. The sex acts pictured made Meri blush and she realized how ridiculous she much look.

"No, sweetling, don't be embarrassed. Everyone has the same reaction when they first enter the club, it really is a stark contrast between old world splendor and the pure decadence that knows no historical bounds." This time her escort tucked her hand in the crook of his elbow and led her down a wide hallway. "I'm Fischer Weston by the way, and I understand that you've met my older brother, Peter." Meri was too surprised by his revelation to comment. She'd heard Peter had a brother with children, but for some reason she'd thought he was older. The man beside her seemed too young to have a family. He leaned down and smiled, "You're right, I am younger than Peter—ten months to be exact. Our parents are very passionate people." She couldn't hold back her giggle at his comment and quick wink. "The rug rats belong to our older brother, Adam." Clearly the two younger Weston brothers were both empaths and Meri wondered if it was a family trait. The gorgeous man holding her arm smiled and replied as if she'd voiced the observation, "Thank you. It is. And here you go."

The door Fischer opened was wide and ornately carved, and the room behind it was enormous. The first thing she noticed that the room before her was an even greater contrast because it bore no resemblance to anything else she'd seen. Cameron Barnes was obviously a man with many facets to his personality because everything in his office was shining steel, sleek lines, and black leather. She knew her surprise showed on her face when she heard Fischer's chuckle, "He wouldn't let me decorate this room. It's not nearly as interesting, is it?" With that he closed the door and she was left facing Cameron Barnes...alone.

CAM ENVIED FISCHER'S effortless ease with everyone he met. Hell, he'd actually thought Fischer was bi when they first met because his ability to connect with both men and women was extraordinary, but he'd soon learned the man's secret. Fischer Weston was one of the most gifted empaths Cam had ever met. All three Weston brothers shared the talent, but Fischer was by far the most gifted of the three.

Cam had to suppress his smile at the bewildered look on Ms. Lanham's face. Fischer often had that effect on people—first they were stunned by his physical appearance and then he literally read their minds, and more often than not it resulted in the very same deer-in-the-headlights look his saw on this sweet sub's face. And there was no question that Merilee Lanham was a submissive, it practically oozed from her pores despite the fact she was recovering quickly and he could practically hear her sharp mind kicking back into gear.

Watching Merilee's spine straighten and her shoulders move back was like watching her don a full suit of armor. Her dazed expression cleared and she zeroed in on him with a laser sharp focus. Cam knew instinctively *this* was the woman that most people saw—the one the donors and foundation employees knew. But he also knew this wasn't the real woman, and he suspected that conflict was part of the reason she'd run. Sure, she'd used the excuse she'd been told her Doms had another woman, but she was far too smart to have not figured out that wasn't true. No, she was fighting the same battle he'd seen countless other highly successful women fight, and for a natural submissive, the struggle was usually epic. It would be fun to watch her fly free of those self-imposed constraints. And there was no doubt her men planned to crash right through all those barriers tonight.

Cam had spoken with Ash and Dex at length earlier in the evening about their plans, and he agreed they needed to storm the walls of her resistance with everything they had because in his experience you only got one shot. Cam had already secured CeCe on the small elevated stage in the bar area, the ruler marks were turning a deep maroon and her bright red ass let everyone in the club know she'd been punished. He didn't plan to leave her there for long, but this public acknowledgment of her bratty behavior would be more of a punishment for his normally perfectly behaved slave than any physical pain ever would. He'd positioned his chair so he could ensure her safety as he'd listened to the men outline their plans. Cam had made a few suggestions and then he'd sent them to the control room to wait. The two men he had watching CeCe would let him know if she became too distressed, but he intended to wrap up this meeting with Ms. Lanham as quickly as possible.

Bringing his thoughts back to the woman standing in front of him, Cam pushed off from his position leaning against his desk and closed the distance between them. Reaching out his hand, he wasn't surprised by her firm handshake. "Welcome to Dark Desires, Ms. Lanham."

"Thank you for your kind invitation, and please call me Meri."

"Well, Meri, your friends were convinced it was time for you to get out a bit, so I was happy to assist. Your Prairie Winds membership allows you to play here but it will require my personal approval." At her surprised look, he simply smiled, "Jax McDonald and I have been friends for many years and he'd have my head on a platter if I didn't watch over you personally." The disappointment in her eyes was easy to read, she'd assumed Ash and Dex had been responsible for the added layer of protection. *You are indeed in for an interesting evening my dear.*

ASH AND DEX watched the monitors in Cam's office as he explained the rules of the club to Meri even though she certainly wasn't going to be alone long enough to need the information. It didn't matter that Trish Jantz was still locked up and the good senator was so busy covering his ass he didn't have time to worry about Meri, they intended to keep a very close eye on their lovely runaway sub. Ash frowned at the fine lines bracketing her pretty green eyes, she obviously wasn't sleeping well, but they'd see to it she slept like a baby tonight. Echoing his own thoughts, Dex leaned close to the screen and cursed, "Fuck, look at the strain around her mouth and eyes. She isn't sleeping well. Damn, I don't sleep worth a shit without her cuddled up against me either." Ash couldn't have agreed more.

Watching Meri place her wrists in Cam's hands made Ash's spine stiffen as his mind screamed *"Mine!"* Even though he knew the cuffs Cam fastened around her wrists were a necessary layer of protection, it still chafed that she was wearing something indicating she was under the protection of another Dom. *Those will come off quickly, I promise you that.* Neither he nor Dex had served with Cameron Barnes, but they had known him for years, so there was a level of trust between them they wouldn't have had in another club. And *that* was the only thing keeping Ash from storming into the man's office, sweeping his wayward woman into his arms, and whisking her away from Dark Desires.

Making their way down the back stairs to wait in the shadows while Cam showed Meri around the club, Ash watched her stilted movements and realized it was the first time he'd seen her look so uncomfortable. It was only then he realized how easily she'd seemed to adapt to whatever social setting she was thrust in to, and that made her unease tonight even more significant. His mom had reminded her four sons regularly that they needed to be the rock a woman could tether herself to in any storm, because women valued feeling safe. *What if this was what Meri had been like before Dex and I came into her life?* Ash remembered hearing Kent commenting on how she had blossomed under their care, but he hadn't asked his friend what he'd meant—he now wished he had.

"She looks scared and insecure. I haven't seen that look on her face for weeks. I don't like it." Dex's words cut straight to the heart of how Ash was feeling as well. They had a clear view of her face when she realized the woman on the small stage was her new friend, CeCe. Meri's eyes widened as she took in the lovely slave's punished back-side. Cam leaned down and spoke to her, no doubt explaining why CeCe had acted out and even from their vantage point, it was easy to see the sheen of tears in her eyes. *Such a soft heart.* Cam moved Meri to the end of the bar, introduced her to the burly bartender and then excused himself to attend to his sweet slave.

Cam had cautioned them to watch her closely before moving in so they knew exactly where her mind was. He and Dex had been Doms for many years, but the one thing they had both learned over the years was they could always benefit from the experience of another Dom. That line of thinking was one of the reasons the Wests held regular training sessions for both Dominants and submissives. All members were encouraged to take advantage of the opportunity to add to their skills, and most did so willingly. Kent often swore the training sessions for subs taught them how to "get around" their Doms because there was usually a whole new rash of bratty behavior after each lesson, but Lilly West had waved off her son's complaint explaining the subs were merely giving the Doms opportunities to practice their new skills and they should be grateful. Even now he had to hold back his chuckle, because the look on Kent and Kyle's faces had been priceless. Their dads had slapped them on the back as if to say, "How did you not see that one coming". Just remembering that moment reminded Ash why he thanked God each and every day that he and Dex had taken Kent and Kyle up on their offer to join the Prairie Winds' team.

For the first time in two weeks, Ash felt himself relax. Hearing Meri say her safe word would always be one of the worst moments of his life. The fact she'd said it had frozen him in his tracks, but knowing Meri had felt the *need* to escape them had rocked him clear to his core. He and Dex had both been blindsided and owed Gracie and Tobi a huge debt of gratitude for helping them keep tabs on their beautiful fugitive. They'd been willing to share information about her recovery, mental state—hell, everything but her location until they'd pushed Tobi for an answer. Both Tobi and Gracie had been willing to share Meri's reason for leaving, but neither of them had been any more convinced of the excuse than he and Dex.

Everyone had assumed the women were communicating electronically while Tobi and Gracie had been working at Dark Desires. None of the men involved were pleased to find out they'd actually been staying with Meri rather than the suite Cam had reserved for them. Tobi pointed out none of them had bothered to actually ask, so she nor Gracie had lied, but Ash knew that hadn't saved her. The little brat knew perfectly well that lying by omission was still lying, but a small part of him had admired her loyalty to her friend. From the thunderous expressions on Kent's and Kyle's faces this morning, Ash was betting sweet Tobi would be sitting on a pillow for most of the coming week. When he realized how far his thoughts had strayed, Ash refocused his attention on Meri and wasn't pleased with what he saw.

Chapter Twenty-Two

STEPPING THROUGH THE door into the club's main room, Meri felt her entire body stiffen. The vibe of Dark Desires was entirely different from Prairie Winds where she felt at home. Oh no, this was a much edgier environment, even before Master C began leading her around the large room she'd known this club was for people whose kinks far exceeded her own. Sure she liked pain because it let her mind soar free, it was a means to an end rather than what she truly enjoyed. None of the Doms she'd scened with had been able to send her into sub-space with pleasure, so she'd used the pain they offered as a way to escape the pressures of her everyday life. But agreeing to pain in a club like this would be an entirely different matter. Sure she had Master C's assurance that he'd look out for her, but what did she really know about the man? *For God's sake, look at CeCe...that says it all.*

Meri wasn't horrified by the bruising on her friend's bare backside—God knew she'd had worse herself, but CeCe's obvious mortification at having her punishment broadcast to the entire club brought Meri's own terror of being humiliated bursting to the surface. It had taken everything in her to not rush to her friend's side. Public humiliation was on Meri's limit list as a hard limit, it was one of the few things she considered non-negotiable. Personally she thought it ranked right up there with bodily fluids and cages, and she felt a shudder of revulsion quake through her. Master C had obviously felt it too because he leaned down and whispered, "I know that she hates being up there, but the lesson is an important one and in the end, pleasing me is what she most desires. If I didn't make it difficult for her, she wouldn't feel as if she'd earned my forgiveness."

When she turned to face him, the sincerity of his words was clearly written in his expression. Meri considered what he'd said before nodding. "How do you know?" When he just raised a brow in question, she continued, "How do you know exactly what she needs? I'm not questioning your judgment, just trying to understand the process better."

"Ahh, the joys of brilliant women—they have such an insatiable thirst for knowledge. Life isn't always a puzzle to be solved, sweetheart. But in answer to your question, it's my job to know what Cecelia needs and to provide it for her even if it's unpleasant for both of us. I enjoyed her punishment because she gives me so few opportunities, but this," he said waving his hand toward the small stage where CeCe was displayed, "well, this is for her not for me. She'll feel as if she'd paid penance and earned my pleasure even though she'd never really lost it. Remember, Doms only have as much power as their submissives are willing to grant them. By its very definition it's an exchange of power, but the situation is stacked heavily in your favor." He tapped the tip of her nose to emphasize his point before settling her near the end of the bar. Master C introduced her to the bartender before quickly excusing himself.

Meri looked on as Master C hoisted himself up on the small pedestal stage with the easy grace of a man who kept himself in superior physical condition. The tenderness in his gaze as he spoke softly to CeCe squeezed her heart and made her long for Ash's and Dex's touch. How was she ever going to be able to forget them? Neither Gracie nor Tobi had answered any of her messages since yesterday, which told Meri their phones had probably been confiscated. And that meant their Doms knew where she was hiding...which meant Ash and Dex knew where she was. *And if they don't want my friends to contact me it's either because Ash and Dex don't care or they're on their way here.* Just the thought of them coming for her sent a moment of joy through her, but then the reality of them finding her in a BDSM club made her reconsider the wisdom of her decision to accept CeCe's invitation.

Suddenly Meri was very curious about that invitation, because a lot of pieces seemed to be falling quickly into place. Her gut told her the invitation hadn't been from CeCe and Meri's message of acceptance had clued CeCe in, which had eventually led to her punishment. And *that* could only mean one thing...

DEX RAN HIS fingers over the slender titanium chain in his pocket and smiled when he reached the hidden locking mechanism. The small heart was engraved with his and Ash's names, and to the casual observer it would look like nothing more than a pretty ornament. But the hidden lock could only be unlocked by two small keys, and those tiny keys now hung on chains around each of their necks. They'd watched Meri's expressions change while Cam tended to CeCe, and even without Fischer's running commentary from beside them, Dex was sure he'd have known how quickly she was processing what had happened.

Fischer had finally said, "Time to move, my friends, and just for the record, that woman's mind is one spectacular place to visit. Be gentle with her tonight because her battle is with herself, not you." Dex wasn't surprised to hear Meri had already figured out Trish Jantz had been lying. What had surprised him was Jax McDonald's input before they'd left Austin. Their friend had explained the challenges women from wealthy families face in personal relationships and how often they are left wondering if a man is interested in *them* or their wealth. Jax's younger sister had the added challenge of being profoundly deaf, making her ability to assess men's motives even more difficult. Considering Meri's recent experience with John Stevens, it was easy to see why she might have doubts.

It was a testament to how deep in thought she was that both he and Ash had been able to step up alongside her unnoticed. The sweet scent of her shampoo filled his nose and Dex felt his entire body respond. In that moment the carefully choreographed plan they'd made dimmed in his mind and the only thing Dex wanted was to be buried balls deep in her glorious heat. Leaning down he whispered against the delicate shell of her ear, "Hello, sweetheart." Her startled squeak made him smile. "We have missed you."

Dex thought they'd planned for every contingency, but her response completely shocked him. Tears were streaming down her pretty upturned face before he'd even finished speaking. Before he could respond, she turned and sank in a graceful slide to kneel perfectly in front of them both. "I've missed you too, Masters. More than I ever thought possible." Even if they'd planned to punish her tonight he would had struggled to follow through. No, she still wasn't healed enough for anything that rigorous so they'd taken a play from the Wests' playbook and decided to be creative. Instead of punishing her, they intended to reinforce her body's recognition of the mind numbing pleasure only they could give her. They wanted to cement the link between themselves and her pleasure. And his throbbing cock was completely on board with the plan and Dex could practically hear it shouting to *"Get on with it, already"*.

Ash and Dex both held out their hands to her, and the feel of her cool fingers in his made him want to lick every inch of her just because he could. Dex watched as his friend stroked the back of his knuckle down her pale cheek, "Talk to us, pet." The tumble of words that came out were so tangled it took Dex a few minutes to realize she'd spilled everything in what had essentially been one sentence. By the time she'd taken a breath, he'd worried she might pass out. "And why didn't you just say that at the hospital instead of your safe word?"

Dex watched Meri take a couple of deep breaths and look between the two of them before slowly looking at the floor, "I don't know. I was so afraid I'd become what John told me so often I was…and the very thought was just too much to even consider."

This time it was Dex who answered, "We'll be dealing with that trust issue someday soon, but not today." He leaned down and pressed his lips against hers, enjoying the sweet taste that was uniquely Meri. "Today is about reminding you how wonderful we are and all the reasons you should never want to run again." Just as he'd hoped, his words broke some of the ice that still seemed to be surrounding them and her shy smile made everything around them seem brighter. Leading her to a corner at the back of the room where Cam had already set up a St.

Andrew's Cross, Dex heard her breath catch at the sight of the Dom whose cuffs she wore. CeCe was wrapped in a soft subbie blanket curled up in the only chair in the small area, Cam obviously wasn't going to prevent members from watching, but he clearly didn't intend to facilitate it either.

CAM CALLED MERI to stand in front of him, which meant her back was to the cross while her men set up. Studying her carefully, he was relieved to see some color in her cheeks and she seemed far more focused than she had when he'd spoken with her earlier. Her condition had almost caused him to call off their plans, but seeing her now, he was glad he'd waited. "Are you alright, sweetheart?"

When she nodded, he raised a brow. He didn't have to wait long before she realized her error and quickly answered, "Yes, Sir, I'm fine."

"I agree that you seem more settled than you were earlier. Is this what you want?" He'd inclined his head to indicate the cross behind her. "This may not be a scene like you are accustomed to, but I think we can all agree you aren't well enough for that just yet." He saw just a tinge of relief in her eyes, but the need in them told him everything he wanted to know. After a few seconds, he nodded, "Good enough, give me your wrists, sweetie." As he unbuckled the cuffs, he whispered quietly, "My lovely slave wants to stay, her mother hen instincts are in full bloom, is that alright?" He wouldn't tell her they'd be staying no matter her answer, better she think CeCe was the reason than know he wasn't willing to set her completely in the care of the two men she'd run from—not yet at least.

"That's fine, Sir. Please tell her thank you and that I appreciate her concern." Cam nodded once and turned her toward Dex and Ash. He returned to scoop his sweet slave up into his arms and settle her on his lap. His heart swelled as she snuggled her face against his neck. For so long he'd been terrified his past would catch up with him, and anyone who saw him with Cecelia would know instantly she was his Achilles' heel. But those fears had never been realized and he'd only recently started letting her out of his sight for anything other than work.

Murmuring sweet words of praise in her ear, he felt the first shivers of arousal move through her. "I promise to give you everything your heart desires, slay all your dragons, and love you until the end of time." She sighed so sweetly and rested her cheek against his chest knowing he'd meant every word.

Chapter Twenty-Three

A SH STEPPED UP in front of Meri and held her chin gently with his fingers, "Pet, rest assured there will be consequences for not trusting us enough to confide your fears, but you won't be punished for using your safe word. That being said, we've come up with a rather unique punishment for you. Are you ready?"

Meri's soft, "Yes, Master," sent the last bit of blood from his brain straight to his cock. Now he just needed to get through the scene without his oxygen-starved brain melting between his ears.

Thankfully Dex had managed to stay focused and when he cleared his throat beside him, Ash took a half step back. "Strip, baby." Ash could see the surprise in her eyes and he wasn't sure if it was the order or Dex's change in the pet name he'd called her. What she would learn soon enough was there was a distinct pattern to the names Dex used. He'd always called her sweetheart, which he considered more of a *boyfriend* name, his use of *baby* let Ash know he was preparing to reel her in.

To her credit, Meri quickly pulled the short wench's dress over her head and handed it to him. Ash heard Dex's growl at the tiny lace thong she was wearing. *No clue what the man has against panties that pretty, hell, they are practically sheer. Seems like a waste to—* His thoughts were cut short by the sound of elastic snapping. "That is the last pair of panties you wear that one of us doesn't hand you, do you understand?"

The sweet scent of Meri's arousal hit him before her soft assent registered. Suddenly feeling almost drunk on the smell of her musk alone, Ash pulled her gently into position and began securing her to the polished wood of the St. Andrew's Cross. The thing was a fucking work of art if you asked Ash. There were hooks for every type of restraint imaginable, there was even an electrical outlet hidden behind a sliding panel on the backside, just in case a Dom decided to use something with a bit more power than batteries could offer. They didn't need those luxuries tonight, hell, his goal was to last until they got her back to her parents' condo, even then the chances of him fucking her against the wall of the glass elevator were better than fifty-fifty.

"You're beautiful, pet. We're going to play a bit before we claim you. Are you ready?" God in heaven, the woman was magnificent. Her skin was even taking on a tinge of color it had been sorely lacking, that rosy glow of a woman's arousal was a total turn on and Ash was humbled to realize how much he missed just looking at her.

Meri's glittering green eyes were dilated and the first hints of her surrender were beginning to show in her glazed expression. When she softly acknowledged his question, he didn't waste a single second before pressing his lips against hers. He'd intended for the kiss to be sweet and inviting, luring her in to their web, but her immediate surrender set off an explosion of need that sent the kiss from sweet to plundering in the time it took his heart to skip a beat. *God in heaven, she undoes me.* Ash had no idea what he'd do if she didn't accept their collar—just thinking about letting her go sent a lancing shard of pain searing through his chest.

Taking her breasts into his hands, Ash rolled her nipples between his fingers. They planned to take her to the piercing specialist as soon as possible, small golden rings through her pretty rose colored nipples would glow beautifully against her tan skin. And a clit ring would sparkle perfectly, drawing the eye to her bare mound and blushing sex. Ash loved the fact she kept herself waxed bare, the smooth skin provided them an unimpeded view and he knew it made her even more sensitive to their touch. Watching her labia swell was like watching a rose blossom in the sun. Pulling himself back to the moment, Ash repeated every Dom's mantra in his head—*Begin with the end in mind.* If they were going to bind her to them, she needed and deserved his full attention…and it was definitely time to *begin*.

DEX LISTENED CLOSELY to the changes in Meri's respirations and was thrilled to hear the quick, shallow breaths that told him she was sliding quickly into the proper headspace. Sliding his hands over her soft shoulders and down her ribcage, he noted she'd lost a lot of weight since being injured at the club—something they'd be dealing with in short order. Her health, both mental and physical, would be a priority. She was a busy woman and she was going to be even busier in the future, so she was going to need her strength. Feeling her shiver at his touch had him leaning forward to kiss the tender spot where her neck and shoulder met. "We'll take care of that need, baby, all you have to do is let go and *feel*."

They would probably make her crazy with their overly

protective personalities, but Dex preferred to think of that particular trait as part of their charm. Sliding his fingers between the wet folds at the apex of her widespread legs, Dex let the tip of his middle finger draw lazy circles around her clit. Pressing kisses up her neck and running his tongue over the outer ridge of her ear he marveled at her responsiveness. "Let us love you, baby."

"Yes, please." Her plea was sweet but lacked the proper ending, and when he heard her sharp intake of breath, Dex knew Ash had pinched her pretty nipples in a silent reminder. "Yes, Master. I want you both, but I'm worried." Dex assumed she was going to say something to confirm Jax's explanation, but she surprised him by adding, "I'm worried I won't be enough." *Enough? She won't be enough? Is she serious?*

He obviously wasn't the only one confused by her confession because he heard Ash's growled, "Enough? Are you fucking kidding me? You're everything we've always dreamed of finding. Stop giving John Stevens so much power in your life. His words were self-serving and don't mean anything other than he was too damned stupid to know what a wonderful gift the Universe had placed in his care." Dex felt her muscles relax again as Ash continued, "Dex and I, on the other hand, know exactly how lucky we are—and we don't intend to let you slip away from us again." Truer words were never spoken, he and Ash wouldn't let her fear keep her from finding the happiness she deserved.

Dex stepped back just enough the pick up the small bullet vibe, butt plug, and remote laying on the small table behind him. Pocketing the remote, he didn't even try to hold back his smile. They'd have her screaming out her release in no time. They'd decided to make sure she was at least partially sated before their little impromptu collaring ceremony, but now that he had his hands on her, Dex would have preferred to just lock the lovely chain in place, wrap her in a blanket, and bolt out the door.

Sliding the bullet vibe through her sweet honey, Dex felt her startle and bit down on the top of her shoulder stilling her immediately, "Stay still, pretty girl, we've brought you a couple of very special toys." He knew she couldn't see the notebook computer to their side, and even though he was anxious to explain all the incredible details of the device he was sliding into her vagina, that was going to have to wait. *Oh, but the sweet joys of having techy friends who are willing to share.* The data sent from the two wireless devices fed incredible amounts of data directly into the computer, which in turn controlled the speed and intensity of the vibrations based on an analysis of the data, keeping a sub on edge for hours if that is what her Master wanted. They didn't plan anything that intense and had really wanted the unique devices simply to free up their hands so they could enjoy every inch of her. They'd been without her between them since the night she'd been stabbed and there wasn't a single square inch of her sweet body they weren't both itching to touch.

Kneeling behind her Dex held the small plug in his hand as he pulled her ass cheeks wide. Her body involuntarily thrust back in invitation and he was more than happy to oblige. Using his tongue to circle her tight hole, Ash gave her a few seconds to relax before slipping the small plug inside. The device was much smaller than either his or Ash's cock but it wouldn't need their girth to launch her into orgasmic oblivion.

The minute he touched the remote, Dex heard her sharp inhalation, "That's right, baby, let those pretty gifts take you higher and higher while we feast on your delectable body." He followed up his words with soft nips to her ass cheeks. Dex knew Ash was ravishing her breasts and just thinking about how gorgeous those nipples were going to look draped in a fine platinum chain with emeralds for weights made his cock twitch and strain against the confines of his trousers.

Dex glanced at the screen when the yellow icon flashed letting them know she was getting close, so he wasn't surprised to hear her soft moan when the two units scaled back their assault. Licking the slick cream from her pussy was a treat and Dex set about the task relishing the pleasure. She was musk and honey all rolled into one and the taste of her on his tongue was testing the limits of his own control.

"Please, Master, I need to come. I don't know how long I can wait." Hearing her soft plea was music to his ears because Dex knew Meri had worried she wouldn't be able to come without pain. Showing her they could send her over with pleasure alone would go a long way to convince her she truly belonged to them.

Hearing Ash's one word command, "Come," set off a chain reaction of response that left Dex in awe of the depth of Meri's submission. As planned, they let her free-fall into orgasm after only two cycles because they knew she was still recovering and certainly didn't intend to wear her out—just wear down her resistance. They'd expected a battle of wills, but had been presented the most treasured gift imaginable—Meri's submission. Her scream was far quieter than usual, likely a lingering effect of her diminished lung capacity, but the huskiness was comforting in its familiarity. The silky flood of cream over his fingers let him ease both the vibe and plug from her trembling body while

Ash released her bonds.

Glancing around him, Dex was shocked to see how large the crowd was that had silently gathered around them. Meri seemed oblivious to them and it pleased him to know she was so focused on them she hadn't even looked around. Ash lowered her gently into a kneeling position and the two men took their position in front of her. Dex could see the first shivers as goose flesh raced over her dewy skin—it was definitely time to get this show wrapped up.

Dex pulled the slender chain from his pocket and when he started to place it around her slender neck, he was surprised to see CeCe and Cameron Barnes standing directly behind Meri. CeCe stoked Meri's hair twice to let her know she was close and then gathered the long locks and held them up. Once the chain encircled her graceful neck, CeCe replaced Meri's long chestnut waves, but they didn't step away. He and Ash each held one end of the chain as they spoke. Their words were for Merilee, but were spoken loud enough for the gathered crowd to hear. Dex was glad Ash was up first, hopefully the extra few seconds would buy him enough time to figure out how to speak around the lump in his throat.

"Merilee, will you accept this collar and everything it stands for?" Ash had used a finger under chin to raise her face so they could look into her eyes. The flash of heat that flared there made Dex's cock jerk in response. *Randy bastard has a mind of his own where Meri is concerned.*

"Yes, Master, it will be an honor."

Dex turned her face ever so slightly toward him, "We promise to cherish, love, and protect you, always. Your submission is a precious gift and not something we'll ever take for granted." Tears shimmered in her green eyes and

Dex felt his heart squeeze with emotion.

This time Ash's voice wasn't as choked with emotion, "We'll have another collaring ceremony when your ring is ready, pet. And of course we'll need to invite all these wonderful witnesses." The room erupted in applause and whistles as they slid the locking mechanism into place. After shaking their hands, Cam handed Dex a soft blanket, which he quickly used to wrap around his sweet sub, hugging her tight enough to make her squeak. Fischer had cleaned their toys and repacked their bag, which he handed to Ash along with his congratulations.

Before they'd even managed to leave the club, both his and Ash's phones had dinged with an incoming message...*You did good!* Tobi's sweet message was accompanied by an animated dancing monkey. He and Ash were both stunned at the little blonde's networking skills—NSA should take note. But the next picture showing Tobi and Gracie holding signs saying *Future Bridesmaids* had he and Ash both laughing out loud. They might be smart as whips, but there wasn't a subtle bone in their bodies. Dex hoped Meri would be just as spirited because he'd seen how much fun the other four Doms had coming up with creative punishments...*Let the games begin.*

Epilogue

C AMERON BARNES DISCONNECTED the call he'd made to Kyle West and stared at his reflection in the enormous mirror hanging in his office. His entire adult life had been dedicated to the study of human behavior. As an operative being able to read body language meant the difference between living and dying nearly every single day. And now, as the owner of one of the world's most successful sex clubs, he used those same skills to help others fulfill their every fantasy.

Cam had started Dark Desires more as a distraction than as a business venture, it had also given him and his friends a safe place to "play" without bringing submissives into their homes. No one had been more surprised by how insanely successful the club had become, but every success has its price.

Becoming a public figure had been a gamble he'd been willing to take because he hadn't had a wife or child at the time. Studying himself in the mirror, he wondered how a man who had seen so much of humanities worst could have become so complacent with the safety of the two people who mattered the most. Ordinarily he didn't believe in regrets—and for a man with his past he had remarkably few. The letter laying on his desk filled with thinly veiled threats to his wife and daughter represented one of the two times he'd completely dropped the ball. The other incident had been twenty-five years ago. And just to prove what an unforgiving bitch she could be, karma was about to steamroll him for both mistakes at the same time. *Serendipity with a twist of fate.*

The End

Books by Avery Gale

The Wolf Pack Series
Mated – Book One
Fated Magic – Book Two
Tempted by Darkness – Book Three

Masters of the Prairie Winds Club
Out of the Storm
Saving Grace
Jen's Journey
Bound Treasure
Punishing for Pleasure
Accidental Trifecta
Missionary Position

The ShadowDance Club
Katarina's Return – Book One
Jenna's Submission – Book Two
Rissa's Recovery – Book Three
Trace & Tori – Book Four
Reborn as Bree – Book Five
Red Clouds Dancing – Book Six
Perfect Picture – Book Seven

Club Isola
Capturing Callie – Book One
Healing Holly – Book Two
Claiming Abby – Book Three

I would love to hear from you!

Email:

avery.gale@ymail.com

Website:

www.averygalebooks.com/index.html

Facebook:

facebook.com/avery.gale.3

Instagram:

avery.gale

Twitter:

@avery_gale

www.ingramcontent.com/pod-product-compliance
Lightning Source LLC
Chambersburg PA
CBHW070620130626
46556CB00001B/424